GALYA

By

Ian Goult

Other books by Ian Goult:

Non-fiction:

Secret Location

Innovation in Hard Times

Make Trauma Redundant – Pseudonym Ewen Gould

Fiction:

Vapour trails

Children's:

Peter and the Giant Octosquid,
A journey into the New World

PROLOGUE

It might be thought that when President Gorbachev came to power in Russia the KGB would have no place alongside Perestroika and Glasnost. Not so. President Gorbachev was an enthusiastic supporter of the activities of the KGB. Although the statue of its founder Felicks Dzerzhinsky no longer stands in Dzerzhinsky Square, the busy headquarters remains under another name. Can such a vast structure with its thousands of officers and agents simply disappear overnight? What will become of the power-hungry elite such as the recently promoted Lieutenant General Ivan Ilyanovitch?

It was from this building that Ivan Ilyanovitch controlled his agents in the countries of the EEC through the trade missions and delegations established in those countries. He travelled through Europe as a senior Minister for the Department of Trade and Industry, but in reality, a member of Directorate T, working in conjunction with the State Committee for Science and Industry, a secret unit of the Academy of Science, its purpose to gather Western technology.

Ivan Ilyanovitch was trained at the tough KGB school in Bolshoi Kiseley Street, just a few blocks away from the KGB headquarters. Here he was taught, along with like-minded students, all the tricks of the trade needed to combat the evil enemies of socialism. They never doubted the righteousness of their cause.

Nor did they question the means by which their cause could be carried forward. The ideology was all. A man's life was in the hands of the state, like his property. Ivan Ilyanovitch dedicated his whole life to the cause with a ruthless efficiency that won the admiration of his superiors.

As he rose through the ranks to his present position so his ambition and taste for the privileges of the elite grew; so, too, did his taste for power, and power he realised lay in the hands of the KGB.

He, with others were plotting the downfall of Gorbachev, then one day on the other side of the Berlin wall capitalism would collapse and with the help of the KGB socialism would take over.

In the meantime, it irked him that in some areas of advanced technology the Soviet Union lagged behind the rest. It was his job to put that right. His network of intelligence agents were spread throughout Europe. However, following the defection of an officer close to the top of the KGB hierarchy there had been mass expulsions of agents from Europe, and London in particular.

Setting up a new trade mission in Europe was the only answer, but where to find agents with a sufficiently broad technical background and a good working knowledge of English? It was possible to fulfil one or other of these requirements, "but where," he asked his mistress, "do you find both?"

"In my old school friend Galya," replied Sonia.

CHAPTER 1

Frank Wigmore looked at the pale faced young lady - or girl, he could not make up his mind which - who had just been introduced to him. It was a formal invitation, so he shook hands with her and sensed her nervousness as he held her hand.

"I have never spoken English to an Englishman before," she faltered in an almost inaudible voice. He smiled at her, desperately wanting to put her at her ease.

"You speak it very well, Galya," he said.

"I am glad you find it so," she responded with obvious relief.

Frank was part of an international conglomerate taking part in a conference in Moscow. There were about thirty in all from the headquarters in New York and associated European houses. He had written a paper to be read at the conference. It had already been translated into Russian and distributed to all the attendees. It was his first visit to Russia and the words Perestroika and Glasnost were not at that time part of the everyday vocabulary.

"I am to translate all the questions from Russian to English," continued Galya. "Then you can write the answers in English, and I will return your answers to the questioner in Russian."

"It sounds a long-winded process."

"Long winded?"

He smiled. "Er, drawn out, tedious. I can't think of the right word."

"I know what you mean. We shall see. I have some questions all ready for you."

"Already! I didn't think there would be any questions until my paper had been read, and that's another two days yet."

"The engineers have had the papers for a week now and I received the first questions this morning. I can translate here when this reception is over."

They were in a large anteroom leading off the conference hall. Frank looked around. The visiting delegates were meeting their hosts. There was a translator attached to each of the visiting delegates, all in earnest conversation. The majority of the translators seemed to be young students or graduates; but the more senior delegates such as the technical director and vice president had mature men attached to them.

Frank's friend, Don had a jolly looking plump girl attached to him. He was already flirting outrageously with her, just as he did with all the female staff back in London. She loved it. How did he get away with it? Frank envied his easygoing ways with women. Admittedly Don started with every advantage, tall, bronzed, athletic, with fair naturally wavy hair and a nonchalant slightly supercilious attitude.

Unlike Frank, Don was still single. He sighed nostalgically. His flirting days were over. There were enough problems with a wife and young family without adding to them. He had seen enough marriages flounder and fail when the husband allowed his eye to roam acquisitively. His marriage was under enough strain already. Engineers were among the poorest paid of all the professions. Edith was always pointing out how well the husbands of her contemporaries were doing, in accountancy, or law or almost any other profession apart from engineering. The comparisons were not flattering. Yet the challenges of engineering were surely the most rewarding - designing a system from concept to fruition - rewarding except financially.

Near to Don was a silver urn like object, from which drinks were being dispensed. "What is that?" asked Frank.

"A samovar, would you like some tea?" She led the way towards it. Frank following saw that she had regained her confidence. Unlike Don's translator she was petite, dressed in a neat white blouse, navy skirt, dark stockings, and sensible black shoes. Her hair was black, and her pale face would have been very ordinary but for her beautiful clear candid eyes. They were looking up at him now as she offered him tea and asked if he would like lemon.

Galya had been terrified at first. What would this Mr. Wigmore be like she had wondered. His paper had not given her much encouragement - very formal, but very clear. She had had no trouble understanding it; but would she understand him. She had spent every evening for weeks listening to the BBC long wave programmes in the flat she shared with her mother. Would he speak as clearly? In the event he did and when they had shaken hands she had sensed his firm encouraging grip. She knew she could cope. All her years of hard work had born fruit. She felt quite light-hearted.

"I'll take lemon and sugar," responded Frank. "I have never seen a samovar before. We don't stew tea in England."

"We do not stew tea," she said, perplexed. "We stew meat."

"But you keep the samovar going all the time," he said, indicating the small flame underneath it.

"Of course. You will be able to have hot tea at any time during the conference."

"Great," he said, taking the cup from her. "I shall need constant sustenance coping with all those questions you have for me." She gave him the ghost of a smile, more with her eyes than her mouth. She was very attractive when she smiled.

Don and his translator joined them at the samovar.

"Meet Lara," said Galya, "we were at college together."

Others joined them and soon a small informal group had formed. Galya introduced Sonia, another old college friend, who was attached to a French delegate, Pierre Molineau. Frank apologised for his poor French. "Don't worry," responded Pierre in perfect English, "You British are all the same. You can never speak any language but your own."

"I only speak a little English," Sonia said slowly with great deliberation.

"Never mind," said Don, "Perhaps I can improve your vocabulary during the next couple of weeks."

"Not a chance," Pierre responded. "I shall be helping her perfecting her French. Not that you don't speak it well already," he added hastily in French. Frank could not help but smile, realising that Don had met his match in the suave and elegant Frenchman.

"It is time we looked at these questions," said Galya.

Frank found it pleasant working with Galya, so serious, so precise. She handed him each question neatly written on separate sheets, each with its own identity number.

"You understand the question?" she asked.

"Oh, I understand the questions all right. It's supplying the answers that is the problem."

"Surely you are a specialist in the subject. You would not be here otherwise."

"You know what they say about specialists. They know more and more about less and less."

"Pah! We say that here too. It is not true. My boss is an expert specialising in aerodynamics and instrumentation, but he is knowledgeable about all things. He has been a great help to me. You have met him."

"Of course; the charming white-haired man who introduced us, but how is it that your boss is an engineer? I thought you were a linguist."

"No, no, I am an engineer. I learnt English at school."

"Remarkable! How did you become so fluent?"

"Reading and listening to the BBC. Books that are banned in Russia can still be obtained from the English library. I have even read From Russia With Love by your Ian Flemming. There are many marvellous English authors. Who could match Charles Dickens, for instance?"

"Who, indeed?" Frank said. He had only managed to persevere with one of Dickens" novels and that was David Copperfield whilst in bed with 'flu. "Do you enjoy engineering?" he enquired.

"No, I was steered into the sciences at school because I was good at mathematics. I would rather have studied the arts."

"So why don't you take up a career more orientated to the arts?"

"Because I am an engineer."

Frank realised that in communist Russia there was no answer to that. "I had better get on with these questions," he said.

After his paper had been read the pressure was off. So long as any remaining questions were answered it seemed pointless hanging about the conference centre, so the little group that had formed went on sightseeing tours of Moscow with the young translators as guides.

They visited the Kremlin. Frank had not realised that it was possible to go inside, but Galya pointed out that the walls simply enclosed the old city. The main government buildings were within the walls and were modern and well guarded, but many of the original buildings remained.

The Armoury, which was in fact a museum, contained all the old Tsarist treasures - diamond studded saddles and swords presented to past Tsars by Sultans and other world rulers, a massive coach on runners in place of wheels for fast winter travel. They were supposed to admire the priceless Faberge Eggs - decorative eggs with embedded diamonds. Why anyone should be pleased with such a useless gift Frank could not imagine.

At the weekend there was an official visit to Leningrad. Frank was prepared to be bored, but bored he was not. Leningrad was a beautiful city owing much to the inspiration of Peter the Great. A statue stood of him astride a horse his drawn sword pointing towards Sweden as if daring them to return. Both the Winter Palace and the Hermitage Museum were initiated by him. The art collection, containing examples of all the masters was so great that in one afternoon it was only possible to view the best of the best.

Frank was getting a new perspective of the world, looking west from the East. They had been attacked from the West for centuries. Napoleon had entered Moscow. Hitler had reached its outskirts. The siege of Leningrad had reduced its population by 250,000, many freezing and starving to death.

If I were Russian mused Frank, I would find the massive show of strength displayed in the Red Square each year greatly reassuring.

Back in Moscow, after an absence of only two days it was like a re-union of old friends as they gathered once again in the conference hall. A full week of activities had been mapped out by the girls.

In contrast to the long drawn out first week the second week passed all too quickly. Frank and Galya without any conscious effort had established a deepening companionship; always glad to be in one another's company. There was no physical contact. That would have ruined it. All too soon it would end and he knew it would be the end of a world he had visited as in a dream, just out of reach, elusive, and never to be recaptured.

Only as they were saying goodbye did he enclose her hand and gently kiss her on the cheek. She was close to tears as he turned and walked briskly to the coach.

CHAPTER 2

Lara got married and seemed set to raise a large family. Sonia was promoted and seemed set for high office in the party hierarchy. Galya shared a flat with her ailing mother and seemed destined to remain her help and companion. Only her interest in the theatre and the kindness of Dr Bronowski made life reasonably bearable. He often asked Galya and her mother to his Dacha in the country. Here Madame Bronowski would take Galya's mother under her wing. Occasionally Alexei, Dr Bronowski's son would join them. Nothing would have pleased his father more than to see Alexei settle down and marry Galya. Galya was always pleased to see Alexei. He was fun to be with, but both sensed his father's desire for them and it created a strain in their relationship. He would sometimes take her to the theatre, but he had other romantic attachments, and, Galya suspected, a mistress in the background.

Galya did not consider a summons to Dr Bronowski's office unusual - a new project perhaps, or a review of an existing one. It was a surprise, therefore, to see a stranger in the office with a very grave and, she sensed a very anxious Dr Bronowski

"Ah, Galya," he said as she knocked and entered, "I would like you to meet Comrade Ilyanovitch from our administrative department." Comrade? Galya's heart sank. It was not that it was in any way unusual, but in the secluded and rarefied atmosphere of the

Aircraft Instrumentation Research Establishment such formalities had long been dropped.

"So this is where you have been hiding your talents," said Comrade Ilyanovitch

"I don't understand, Comrade," she responded awkwardly.

"I have a very good report of your work. It is time it was recognised. You are due for promotion and advancement."

"But I am very happy here." She looked anxiously at Dr Bronowski.

"And I have been very happy to have had you in my team. I shall be sorry to lose you."

"You mean I shall be leaving the department?"

Comrade Ilyanovitch smiled at her, but there was no warmth in the smile.

"Yes," he said. "You see, my dear, you have an additional all too rare expertise - your proficiency in English." She should have felt flattered, but she had a sense of foreboding. No good could come of this man. "We are increasing our Trade Mission in London, and you are to join it."

"I can't," she burst out desperately. "I have to look after my mother."

"Your mother would be better looked after in a Home. That is being arranged."

*   *   *

"What are you doing to me," screamed her mother, when Galya returned to the flat. "How could you consign me to a Home?"

15

Galya stared at her in horror. "Mother, you surely don't believe I could suggest such a thing."

"Why not? Why else did you lean English? Why else did you read all those English books and listen to the BBC programmes? Oh yes, I should have seen it coming. You are a deceitful little hussy. Your father was just the same. He was a clever man. We could have lived a privileged life, with a dacha in the country among all the important people who matter and have influence; but oh no, he wasn't going to join the party, get to know the right people and use influence to get on, so he got left behind. He was so stupid."

"Stop it Mother. You know how I loved Dad. He was the kindest and gentlest of men."

"Was it kind to let us rot because of his stubbornness?"

"Mum, you know it wasn't stubbornness. He told us of the cruelty of Stalin's collective farm programme. He wanted no part of it. He was right. Stalin has been shown for the tyrant he was. I am glad Dad distanced himself from those men.

"And glad I am going into a home, no doubt."

"No. Mother, you really must believe me. I did try to explain to Comrade Ilyanovitch that you needed me here, but it was no use, it was all decided.

There was a knock at the door. Galya opened it.

"Alexei! Am I glad to see you." Alexei took her hand and squeezed it.

"Father told me what has happened." He went over to Galya's mother knelt down beside her and took both her hands in his. Father has been able to use his influence to get you into a sanatorium that is reserved for the dependants of the senior government officers. It is very well appointed, and mother will be visiting often to see how you are getting on."

Galya's mother burst into tears again and then dabbing her eyes said, "I suppose it is for the best. It is time I pulled myself together."

It was three weeks later when Alexei accompanied Galya to the airport. He had been her constant companion during this time. "Don't waste a minute of your last weeks in Moscow," he had said. She had been given a generous advance on expenses in hard currency with instructions from comrade Ilyanovitch to smarten up her drab wardrobe.

"There will be generous expenses in London," he had said. "I want you to be a credit to our country while you are there." With this in mind she did an absolute minimum of shopping in Moscow, finding the hard currency was a passport to all the concerts and theatres she had had so much difficulty getting to before. Alexei had been her willing escort in these forays into the nightlife of Moscow, wining and dining among the tourists and privileged.

After her mother had moved to the sanatorium, where the company and companionship of the staff and patients was already doing more good than any treatment,

Galya stayed as a guest of Dr. Bronowski and his wife.

"I am going to miss you," Alexei said as they waited at the airport for Galya's flight to be called.

Galya smiled up at him. "I've enjoyed these last few weeks. You and your father and mother have been good to me since my mother went to the sanatorium. I really am grateful."

"No need for thanks. It is only now that you are leaving that I have come to realise just how much I am going to miss you. You are the loveliest and sweetest girl I have ever met."

"And you have met quite a few, haven't you?"

"That makes me all the better judge," he replied, quite unabashed.

"Idle flattery. I have been around all the time. Until now you have hardly noticed me."

"That is the trouble. You have always been around. I have been blind. I have taken you for granted - because you have always been there. Now I wish you weren't going. I would make it up to you. You would be the only one."

"I'm coming back, I promise. They are calling my flight." In a single swift movement she picked up her cabin bag, raised herself on tiptoe, kissed him lightly on the lips, turned and disappeared through the PASSENGERS ONLY door.

Alexei stood staring after her.

CHAPTER 3

The Ilyushin 62 accelerated along the runway, lifted its nose and left Russia behind. Galya looked down at the receding ground with a mixture of anxious anticipation and excitement, the familiar behind her, the new and unknown before her. She knew nothing of her new duties. She would be met at Heathrow Airport and her job would be outlined at the London Location. It would not be at the embassy. The trade mission was at a separate location. What could she do at a trade mission? Her life had been cloistered. She knew nothing of the wider activities of her department, if, indeed, she was still in that department.

"Would you like a drink before lunch, Madame?" Galya looked up at the airhostess in surprise. She had addressed her English.

"I…I am Russian," she stammered.

The airhostess blushed. "I do beg your pardon, Comrade. I did not have time to check the passenger list. I am used to this compartment being taken up with English or American businesspeople."

"This compartment?" Galya had been faintly aware that the seats behind her were all taken. The seat behind her was still vacant, as were several seats in front of her. She also realised that a curtain she had not noticed before had been drawn across. She was in front of that curtain. However, her concern was for the airhostess, who was no older than herself believed she had given offence to a very important person. Galya smiled up at her. "Don't worry," she said. "I was surprised. I suppose I am in the right compartment?"

The airhostess laughed. "If you are not there is nothing, we can do about it. The rear compartment is full. Let me check your boarding pass." She looked at it thoughtfully. "You are in the right compartment. Will you have a drink - complements of Aeroflot?"

"Thank you, just a fruit juice."

So I travel first class in a classless society, mused Galya. She gazed down at a sea of white clouds as they climbed into the clear blue sky - in limbo between two worlds. She ordered half a carafe of red wine with her lunch and a Cointreau with her coffee. She sighed, realising that all too soon she would be coming down to earth.

They broke cloud over the coast of Suffolk. Her first view of England was reassuring - open country as far as the eye could see. No sign of the urban sprawl she had expected in such an overpopulated country. They continued to descend approaching London from the northeast, turning onto the approach over the city itself. The aircraft banked and she recognised, from photographs she had seen, Buckingham Palace and the Houses of Parliament. All too soon they were skimming over the runway threshold and were down.

Her heart sank as she entered the arrivals concourse from the customs area. How could she possibly find who was to meet her; and how could anyone pick her out from the hundreds of passengers streaming out with her? There were people holding up placards with names on. Not the Russian way, she thought and was right. Her name was not among them. She felt very alone. A taxi to the Russian embassy would no doubt solve the problem, if they acknowledged her. It might be better to "phone first. She followed the signs to the telephone.

"Galya, Galya," called a strangely familiar voice. Galya swung round.

"Sonia! Am I glad to see you? What are you doing here?"

"Looking for you, of course. You were getting worried weren't you?"

"I was, but what are you doing in London?"

"I am attached to the trade mission. I have been here nearly a year now. I am beginning to feel like a native. Put your case on this trolley. My car is in the car park."

"Your car?"

"Yes it is essential for getting about, if you are here for any length of time. You will be getting yours soon."

"I can't drive."

"We'll fix that. In the meantime, I had better ring to say you have arrived safely. You needn't go into the office. I will show you around a bit."

"Will that be all right?"

"Yes, if I say so." Galya, was about to comment, but thought better of it and checked herself. Sonia, she realised, was making statements, not inviting comment. "Stay by your case while I "phone or the bomb squad will come to blow it up."

Sonia returned from phoning. "All sorted," she said. "We might as well go straight to my flat where you can unpack and relax. You are staying with me for the moment - more convenient than a hotel?"

"You have your own flat?" Galya could not check herself.

"Yes. Now let's go to the car. Follow me across the footbridge. I was able to park on this level so it isn't far."

Further conversation was impossible as they weaved their way across the crowded concourse and across the pedestrian bridge to Sonia's car, a silver-grey Mercedes. It looks new, Galya thought, putting her case in the boot. As if reading her thoughts, Sonia said, "It's not new. It's about two years old."

"And it's yours?"

"Sort of," said Sonia vaguely as they got into the car.

Galya remembered the vivacious friend of her college days. Had she changed? Not on the surface, but there was a change, a subtle change she could not place. She had matured and advanced whist I have stood still, cloistered in my academic world, concluded Galya. "Where is your flat?" she asked as they entered the outskirts of London.

"St. John's Wood. It's close to Swiss Cottage underground station for easy access into central London, shopping and the theatres."

Sonia laughed as she saw the perplexed look on her friend's face. "It might have been a wood once. Swiss Cottage takes its name from a nearby Pub. We might go out to a Pub for a meal tonight. I hate cooking, and Pubs are good places to meet the natives. The cooking can be your department now."

"Thanks a lot. So far I have heard of nothing but sightseeing, theatres, shopping, cooking and eating in Pubs. Will I have time to do my job, whatever that may be?"

"That is part of your job, apart from the cooking."

"That is ridiculous. Do you know what my job is? I was told I would be informed by my Head of Department in London."

"I certainly do know what your job is. I am your Head of Department."

CHAPTER 4

"We are going shopping," announced Sonia at breakfast. You need to extend your wardrobe. Part of your job will be our official representative at engineering and technical conferences and seminars. This will take you all over the country, as far afield as Edinburgh University in Scotland and other places all over the UK. You will be able to travel more freely than members of our diplomatic corps at the Embassy. They are confined to the Greater London area by the British Government."

Galya would have liked to question Sonia more, but she would not be drawn further. She was pleased and relieved that her old school friend was her boss. There was little doubt however that it was Sonia's intention to control her in her own way and in her own time.

"First, we will go to Oxford Street, said Sonia. There's a Marks & Spencer there where we will get all the underwear we need." And Sonia made sure she was set up, despite all Galya's protests that she had never had so many clothes in her life.

After lunch they went to Knightsbridge where Sonia did some shopping for herself, buying an outfit at a price that Galya realised, despite her inexperience with British currency, was very expensive. "I have an account here," Sonia explained, "so we might as well get you one or two really smart outfits and cocktail dresses. I have also made an appointment with the hairdresser here. I need a set and you are having a perm."

"You're the boss," said Galya. She felt she was being swept along on a wave over which she had no control.

Back at the flat Sonia kicked off her shoes, settled on the settee and tucked her legs under her. She had rustled up sandwiches and coffee telling Galya to take the opportunity to have a shower and freshen up.

Suitably refreshed Galya sat at the table with her coffee. Sonia spoke.

"Now let us get back to your job. First Secretary."

"First Secretary?"

"Yes. It is a rank carrying sufficient prestige to enable you to mix and meet with senior industrialists and academics on an equal footing and as I said last night you will be attending conferences and seminars all over the UK."

"In certain areas of technology," continued Sonia, "we lag behind the West. In your area of specialised instrumentation and automatic test equipment for instance."

"Surely not," Galya bristled. "Dr Bronowski is brilliant and acknowledged to be without equal in his field; and weren't the Russians the first to pit a sputnik into orbit."

"That was a magnificent feat, but the sophistication of the American space craft that followed made our efforts look crude, particularly in the areas of instrumentation, data gathering and automatic control. Your dear Dr. Bronowski is only ahead of his field in Russia."

"Only because he hasn't been given the resources to make full use of his talents."

"Precisely, but even if he was given unlimited resources we are so far behind that it would take years to catch up the West. This is true not only in your specialised areas, but across the board, especially in computer and microprocessor technology."

"So we are spies."

"Don't be so crude. We are doing no more than the Japanese have been doing for years. The Germans used to make the best cameras in the world. The Japanese copied them and now they lead the world."

"Your job," continued Sonia, "is to attend conferences and exhibitions relating to advanced technology and pick up legitimate data. This will be sent, along with other data obtained elsewhere, back to Russia where it will be collated and analysed. Every bit of information, which may be useless on its own, when integrated into all other scraps of information begins to form a complete picture."

"You are also to talk to as many people as possible to try to pick up additional information that might not be generally available. You will have a desk at the trade mission where you will be able to co-ordinate and collate all the information you have gathered into a form that can be processed."

"I am not sure I want to thank you for getting me involved in all this," Galya said, looking accusingly at Sonia. "I still don't know why I was chosen. You can't have believed it was the sort of thing I would want to do - the spying I mean."

"No, quite frankly, I didn't. I wish you wouldn't call it spying. We don't get involved with covert operations unless we are really desperate for a missing link or gap in the information and you are most unlikely to be involved with such operations."

"But they do go on."

"Of course."

"I don't like it. Some of the information you are after will be sensitive military weapon details."

"No, our department is primarily concerned with industrial data, but there is bound to be some overlap."

"Are you part of the KGB?"

Sonia hesitated. "They are a political organisation. Our interests are commercial. Occasionally we find ourselves on common ground. Let us get back to your work. Our organisation operates worldwide. Most of the technology we require originates in the United States; but they have very strict regulations in order to prevent it from passing into what they regard as undesirable hands, meaning us. To them we are the enemy."

"How stupid."

"It stems from our glorious revolution. Originally, you remember, it was to be a world revolution. They never got over the fright. They were hell bent on destroying it. That put us on the defensive. Hence the arms build up."

"Stupid."

"Maybe, but that is the way it is. If we are behind in certain areas of technology I would have thought you would want to put it right whatever the political ramifications."

"When you put it like that it does not seem so bad."

"You are getting the idea. The Americans permit more of their advanced technology products to go to their allies than they would consider safe to pass to us. That is why we are so active in Europe. We do well in France and Italy. There is a need to do more here. It was while I was discussing this with Ivan that I mentioned that I had an old school friend of mine who was pretty bright and had a good command of English."

"Ivan?"

"Comrade Ivan Ilyanovitch. He stays here when he comes to the UK, which is as often as he can."

"Oh no!"

"What's wrong? Don't you like him?"

"I hate him."

"I love him; or perhaps I should say he loves me. You might have notices I have a double bed in my room."

"Sonia, how could you?"

"Quite easily. I know he is not much to look at, but he's really something in bed. I like a man who knows what he is about. Don't look so disgusted."

"I am disgusted. Does your career mean so much to you? You just admitted you don't love him. It wouldn't be so bad if you did. Don't you ever feel you would like to settle down and get married, set up a home and have children?

"Sometimes, but I resist it. If I did, I could not live as one of a crowd in a tenement block. It would have to be someone who really was someone, someone near the top. That is where I am aiming for, one way or another. Stop diverting me. Where was I?"

"You were telling me you mentioned my name to the man that made you his mistress."

"Oh, yes. So when he made enquiries he found he had struck gold. You were working on automatic test equipment, using the latest computer technology, programming in machine and high level languages and had a working knowledge of English. Perfect for the job. We have too many agents who are specialists in a narrow field and have language difficulties. You will be able to get so much more out of the conferences. As you gain confidence, you will be able to talk to delegates on equal terms. This will take time. In order to gain confidence you will have a roaming commission, calling at the office only when necessary to make a report."

"You can go and visit the libraries of the various engineering institutions, going about London at will, getting the feel of the place. I will be coming along with you for the first few days. I will show you the business and better class areas. London is not as safe as Moscow. If you find yourself in a place you are not happy about call a taxi and get back this way. The underground system is safe during the day. At night use taxis. You will have a generous allowance."

"One of your first tasks will be to locate computer software and hardware distributors. Find out what is worth having, but not available in Russia. Purchase it. If you can pay cash you will be able to take it away. I can arrange transport when necessary or give you an address where heavy items can be sent. Is it beginning to make sense?"

"I suppose so."

"You don't sound all that enthusiastic."

"How involved is Comrade Ivan in all this?"

"There is no need to worry about him. I said I would be looking after you. He was quite taken with you. You made quite a hit."

"I can't imagine why."

"It's those lovely wondering eyes of yours and your trim little bum. I will have to watch it or I will be losing my Ivan."

"No need to worry on that score."

"I am not so sure. If Ivan wants something he usually gets it one way or another."

CHAPTER 5

To say that Edith Wigmore was fed-up would be an understatement. Why did she have to marry an engineer?

"Hello dear, sorry I'm late." Frank came into the kitchen and pecked his wife on the cheek. She made no response.

"I know," she said, "you have been to a meeting, and it went on longer than expected. The dinner is ruined - as usual."

"I don't enjoy meetings. In fact, I hate them."

"Somebody must enjoy them. Otherwise, you wouldn't have so many."

"Some people have nothing better to do. It is the new fashion of running research and development programmes with professional managers. They come straight out of Business College fussing about with PERT charts, critical path analysis, milestones, and target dates. What I want are good engineers under me to get on with the job, not Programme Managers telling me what to do. We have meetings to plan the job, meetings to review the plan, progress meetings, meetings to discuss problems raised at the progress meetings; then to cap the lot meetings with the ministry, who are the paymasters and expect a damned good lunch out running well into the afternoon, after of course we have had meetings to decide tactics for the ministry meeting."

"Yes dear. Mary's husband is a Programme Manager - such a charming man. He is to be captain of the Golf Club next year."

Frank finished his meal in silence.

Sally, his youngest daughter came bursting into the room. "Dad, will you do my maths for me. I can't understand the questions."

"No. I won't do them for you. I will help you understand them. You will never learn if you don't have a go."

"Don't be so mean," snapped his wife. "She has an essay to finish, and then she should go to bed."

"Then what I will do is sketch out the answers with explanations."

"Thank you, Daddy." Sally gave him a big kiss.

"Cupboard love. Will you crew for me at the sailing club on Saturday?"

"No she will not," intervened her mother. "You are bound to capsize again and then we will have her at home with a cold."

Sally giggled. "You were cross," she said. "Dad wanted to continue the race after we had righted the dinghy, but you were shouting so much from the bank he had to come back."

"That will do," said her mother. "You couldn't go anyway. I have asked the Robinson's to tea.

"Then Dad's sure to go sailing."

"Get back to your homework, young lady."

After Sally had left Edith said, "It's all right for you to swan off sailing when we can't even afford a holiday."

"It's not as expensive as the Golf Club."

Perhaps if you belonged to the golf club you would meet influential people who could help you, and if you sold your boat we could have a holiday."

"All right, I will sell the boat. I had hoped we could go to the club as a family. Other kids crew regularly and have a lot of fun together. There always seems a good reason why ours can't go."

"I wish you wouldn't call them kids. It's so common. Why is it that everyone else can have expensive holidays but us?"

"I did warn you that if we sent Sally and Kate to a private school it would be tight financially."

"It's not tight for other parents. Why don't you get a decent job?

"I have a decent job. I am an international authority in my field."

"So why don't they pay you more? Bob Chapple is an accountant. I do meals on wheels with his wife. They have just moved into a four bed-roomed house. He must be earning nearly twice your salary. I suppose you resent that. Success is a dirty word to you."

"Yes I do resent it. Accountants are good at telling businesses where to make economise, but stifle expansion. They should advise, not run a business. They kill it."

"Sour grapes. What about Jessie's husband? He is something in the City. They are loaded."

"Shuffling money around to no very good purpose. A company investing in research for long time growth instead of paying high dividends sees the share price fall and is in danger of being taken over by some money grabbing financial institution unable to see beyond the next half year figures."

"It is a pity some of that attitude doesn't rub off on you. You hate anything that makes money. I hate you. I really hate you. I don't know how the children can hold their heads up at school.

Frank got up and left the room.

It was with a heavy heart that he made his way to Brighton for the British All Electronics Show. There was no particular reason for him to go this year. It was more force of habit and an excuse to get out of the house for a couple of days. He had neglected to tell Edith that he had not booked for any of the seminars that accompanied the show. She had assumed that he would be staying away for the night. He had asked his secretary to book him a room at The Queens Hotel - the firm would be paying.

He drove along the deserted front towards the conference centre. The sea was a dull grey, reflecting the low overcast clouds above. The massive waves rolled relentlessly in towards the shore appearing to rear up as they broke and crashed onto the beach sending spray across his windscreen. He shivered. First priority coffee.

He entered the brightly lit, busy conference hall with relief, left his coat in the cloakroom and made for the coffee bar. Coffee in plastic cups? Oh, well, it was still coffee. He sought out an empty table and made his way towards it. A smart young woman or was it a girl approached the table. Damn, the last thing he wanted was to have to make polite conversation.

At the table their eyes met. Galya gasped, spilling her coffee on the chair she was about to sit on. "Let me get you another chair," said Frank pulling round a spare chair from the next table. He sat down opposite. "Galya it's good to see you again. What are you doing here?"

She put both her arms on the table, looked up to him with the ghost of a smile and said, "the same as you. I am attending the exhibition."

"All right then. What are you doing over here?"

"I sometimes wonder myself. I am attached to the Soviet trade mission. At the moment I am looking for test equipment for our research laboratories. There is such a mass of it I don't know where to start. Perhaps you could help me."

"I'll try. You could ask me some questions and I will see if I can answer them. I seem to remember that we did that once before."

"That would be nice."

Frank took her round some of the relevant stands and introduced her to some of the representatives he knew. It began to get crowded.

"Let's get out of here," he said. "I'll take you to lunch."

"Isn't it a bit early. I would love a walk by the sea first."

"It's pretty windy out there."

"I'm not made of cotton wool. I have a wind cheater in the cloak room."

"This is great," said Galya leaning into the wind getting sprayed by the breaking waves. I love the sea. I suppose it is because I'm so far away from it in Moscow."

"You must love it to be down here in a full-blooded gale."

"You don't mind?" asked Galya anxiously.

"Mind? Not likely. I'm loving it too - for a different reason."

"I'm so glad," she said, slipping her hand into his.

"Yes, I have felt lonely and friendless over here," Galya said in answer to a question from Frank. They were drinking coffee in the lounge of a hotel overlooking the sea, after a leisurely lunch. She had told him of the events leading to her transfer to London. "Of course, I am lucky to be sharing a flat with Sonia, but she is very busy and preoccupied. At work she is very formal, being head of a large department. She is an efficient administrator. She does relax a bit in the flat, and we get on well together, despite my bad cooking."

"Have you seen much of London?"

"Not nearly as much as I would have liked. That's what I mean by being lonely. It's not much fun sightseeing on your own. Most of the staff are male and have their wives here - to keep them out of mischief."

"I've got some holiday in hand, and Edith doesn't seem to want my company. Would you like me to show you round?"

"There's nothing I'd like better."

"That would be wonderful."

Have you anywhere particular in mind?"

"Oh yes. There's the House of Commons, St Paul's Cathedral, the British Museum, the Tower of London, Windsor Castle. Then there are the theatres, Covent Garden, The last of the Proms…"

"That will do to be going on with. We'll start Monday. No. We will start this afternoon. I will take you to see Prinnie's Palace."

"What on earth is that?"

"The Brighton Pavilion; where the Prince Regent entertained his mistress."

"Sounds fascinating."

"I will have to go back to fetch my car," said Frank as they were leaving the Pavilion.

"Good, we can walk back."

"You are a glutton for punishment. Haven't you done enough walking for one day?"

"No. It will do you good. You have put on weight since you were in Moscow."

"Maybe, but you don't need to watch your weight. You have a figure as lithe as one of those Russian gymnasts."

"Perhaps that is because I am one."

"What? You never told me."

"Why should I? I represented my college and was short-listed for the Olympics, but you have to be really good. I wasn't that good. They were really something. I sometimes trained with them. Now I keep fit by walking." She slipped her arm in his and they set off at a brisk pace, laughing as the wind howling past them did its best to lift them off their feet.

"Where are you staying?" asked Frank.

"Queens Hotel. I could have returned to London tonight, but Sonia persuaded me to stay. I have an idea she is entertaining a guest. I didn't enquire too deeply."

"Good I can entertain a friend tonight. I am staying at the Queens too.

"It is dinner you are talking bout?"

"Of course."

"How is it, Galya, that between some people there is a natural rapport - no strain? Two strangers from completely different backgrounds feel completely at home with one another." Dinner had taken the whole evening. They were still in the dinning room. "Darling Galya, I'm in love with you - real old-fashioned love. You have taken my heart. I have to tell you. I can't keep it bottled up. I hope I haven't embarrassed you."

"Of course not, Frank. I felt your - how can I say - your concern for me the very first time we met; when I was so nervous. I felt I could trust you, and I was right. Love? I'm not sure. I value your friendship. I too feel that sense of rapport. How else could we talk like this now? But Frank," she smiled up at him, her eyes mocking him, you have been mentally undressing me during the meal, haven't you?" He blushed. He had indeed. He had seen a petite neat figure with small firm breasts, devoid of droop, and beautiful candid eyes meeting his without a flicker, just as they were now. He wanted to hold her close, tenderly, protectively.

"Yes," he said. "It's your fault. You are too damned attractive, but believe me, Galya, it isn't only that I find you physically desirable. I love you for the lovely person you are. I would like nothing better than to be with you always."

"Frank, don't be offended, when I give myself to anyone it will be a total commitment. It could be with someone like you. I am more down to earth than you. You have responsibilities and ties. There would be a conflict, even though your marriage is a sham. I know by the way you talk of your children that you care for them, which is as it should be of course, and you wouldn't want to desert them at such a critical time of their lives. Am I right?"

"You are very perceptive. If only we had met earlier."

"We didn't, so let's make the best of the situation as it is. We are good friends who like each other's company, and you are going to show me round London - OK."

Frank laughed. "OK. Let's drink to that.

CHAPTER 6

"Hello," said Sonia, as Galya burst into the flat. "You look particularly radiant after your dull old exhibition."

"Guess who I met?"

"Tell me."

"Frank Wigmore. Do you remember him? I was his translator a few years ago at a symposium. He was at the exhibition. He gave me a lift back."

"That was nice. Will you be seeing him again?"

"Oh yes. He has asked me to crew for him on Sunday. He goes dinghy racing. It sounds exciting. I need to buy a wet suit. Apparently, the slightest error of judgement will tip you into the drink."

"Sounds great."

"And he is helping me with contacts for automatic test equipment."

"Good, you want to cultivate him." Sonia was more pleased than she could admit. She had had a letter through the diplomatic bag from Comrade Ilyanovitch that was a little disturbing. He was pleased with the reports he had received from Galya as far as they went but made it plain that it was time, he was receiving data on advanced military technology.

"He has a lot of contacts throughout the industry," continued Sonia. "There is information that is a little more difficult to get."

"Such as?"

"Infrared photographic surveillance photographic equipment for Tornado aircraft. This is all new work that is going on and is surrounded in secrecy. We need to know what is going on in these and other similar fields."

"I don't think Frank would let me have any confidential or secret information."

"You might be able to persuade him. Use your charm. That is why you are here. You have had it easy so far."

"This is what I suspected from the start. You are part of a spy operation."

"Don't be so damned sensitive. It's information you are after and if you can't get it one way you will have to try another. I thought you might meet up with your old friend. That's why I sent you to Brighton."

Galya bit her lip. She could have wept with frustration. Her meeting with Frank had turned sour.

Sonia saw her friend's discomfiture. She was annoyed, as much with herself as with Galya. She should never have mentioned her to Ivan. She was part of another world. Try as she might, she was too fond of Galya to be severe with her. Dammit, she actually felt protective towards her. She wouldn't push it far the moment. Let Galya get more involved and then she might take a hand herself. She put her arm round Galya's shoulder. "All right, don't worry about it. Just ask him if he could help. See what his reaction is."

"I will do what I can. You are under pressure yourself, aren't you? It is all so stupid - all this subterfuge. Wouldn't it be better to co-operate, rather than aim for world revolution, which is most unlikely now anyway, then we wouldn't need espionage, military or otherwise."

"You are an idealist."

"I thought it was the Marxists that were supposed to be the idealists."

"Perhaps with all this talk of perestroika and glasnost your dream will come true; but I doubt it. The KGB is still a power to be reckoned with. With the best will in the world you cannot dismantle a structure like that, even if you wanted to."

"They managed it in Poland and East Germany, even Czechoslovakia,"

"It's early days yet."

Frank arrived early on Sunday morning to pick up Galya. Sonia took the opportunity to open the door to him. "Come in, Come in Frank. Galya isn't ready yet."

Galya had been too preoccupied having a hilarious time showing off her wet suit to have noticed Sonia's preparations, which had been unusually elaborate for a Sunday morning. She had put on a close-fitting housecoat, done up just sufficiently to show the right amount of leg as she moved.

"Nice to see you again, Sonia. You look as beautiful as ever." He moved towards her intending to kiss her lightly on the cheek, but Sonia, with a deft movement of her head, kissed him on the lips. He was aware of the subtlest waft of perfume.

"You are looking pretty good yourself," she replied. "Have a coffee while you are waiting."

"I'll be out in a minute," called Galya from her room. "I have been trying out my wet suit."

Sonia poured the coffee and cleared the remains of breakfast.

"You needn't have bothered with a wet suit," Frank said. Do like me and take a change of clothing. If we capsize, we come in to dry and change."

"That would mean we couldn't finish the race. We are going to win today."

"You're hopeful, with me as helmsman and a novice crew. I've never won yet."

"You've never had me to crew. I've been reading all about it. It's all about balance."

"Yes, and you will need all your gymnastic expertise hanging out on that trapeze if the weather forecast is correct. It will be gusting to force 5, so with your light weight you will be out at full stretch most of the time." He had had second thought about the wisdom of allowing her to crew. Her enthusiasm reassured him.

"I trust you will come back and spend the evening with us," purred Sonia.

"You forget I have a home to go to. Some other time perhaps."

Sonia pouted her lips in mock disappointment. "Arrange things better next time," she said.

Frank laughed. "You tempt me. I'll see what I can arrange," he said.

"I'll keep you to that," said Sonia. Galya didn't look pleased.

Galya came out of the changing room at the club wearing the top of her wet suit only. "The trousers are too restricting," she explained.

"You look every inch an athlete," responded Frank. On an impulse Galya did a quick aerial somersault, landing perfectly upright.

"Bravo," called a chorus of voices from the club hut. "Can you do that again?"

Galya looked in alarm at the hut; then, seeing the funny side of it, made two further somersaults in succession.

"Can you do cartwheel?" asked David Stevenson, the club secretary and national fireball champion, coming out of the hut. Galya blushed, and not knowing any other way of coping with the situation, decided to comply. "Can you find me a crew like that?" continued David."

"No," said his attractive wife behind him. "You have a good crew already."

Frank laughed and introduced Galya to the rest of the club, among much ribbing that he would give her ducking before the day was over.

They rigged and launched the boat, and went for a trial sail before the first race. Frank was surprised how quickly Galya appreciated the setting of the sails for any wind condition. "It's obvious," she said. "It is just a matter of practical aerodynamics to get the maximum pulling power and optimum venturi effect from the slot between the jib and mainsail, then preventing the boat from healing over by hanging out on the trapeze as far as necessary"

"Right, and if we can keep upright when there is a good gust the boat will rise and plane on top of the water instead of ploughing through it."

"Let's try it then."

Frank sailed to get the wind on the beam. As the boat gathered speed he drew in the mainsheet and Galya followed by drawing in the jib easing herself out on the trapeze as she did so. The hull lifted" spray flew out from either side and there was a further exhilarating burst of speed.

The ten-minute hooter went, and they sailed back to the starting line.

The first race was a disaster from the start. In his anxiety to stay out of trouble in the melee of boats jockeying for the most favourable position with a novice crew, he was last across the start line. However, on the downwind leg he had the best of the wind, and with his lightweight crew was able to move past some of the other tail enders.

"At least we weren't last," said Frank, as they tied up at the jetty, "and we didn't capsize."

"No, and we could have won."

"How do you make that out?"

"We overtook half the fleet, didn't we?"

"True,"

"So if we had started among the leaders we might have overtaken them. With our light weight, particularly mine, we will rise and plane sooner, pass to windward and give them our dirty wind."

"Your logic is impeccable. It's the realisation in practice that is in doubt."

"We can try."

"We can. David always manages to get a good position at the starting line. I will try sticking to his tail before the starting gun. It will mean sailing aggressively behind the starting line immediately before the gun."

"Let's do that. Your crew is more experienced now."

After a quick snack lunch they practised continuously, learning to work as a team. At the start of the afternoon race Frank knew he could rely on his crew to respond to any situation. He was on David's tail at the stating gun. David rounded the first mark leaving no room for Frank to get between his boat and the buoy. The next mark would be approached on the port tack. Frank turned wide of the course to the mark and well to the lee of David, rising to plane before him and drawing in the sheets to come back close hauled was able to call "mast abeam" allowing him to luff up closer into wind forcing David to do the same. It was now that the lighter weight of frank and his crew were at their full advantage, for as David pulled into wind to allow for Frank's manoeuvre, he came off the plane and Frank moved ahead. Knowing how much Galya wanted to win Frank sailed as he had never sailed before with Galya anticipating every slight movement of the boat as though she were part of it.

As they sped across the finishing line Galya flung her arms into the air. "We've won, we've won," she cried. "I told you we could." With the jib now flying out of control Frank could no longer hold the boat steady and it healed beyond the point of no return depositing both of them into the water.

Showered, dried, and changed they were talking to David and his wife in the clubhouse. "That was an inspired bit of sailing," David was saying. "You and Galya make a wonderful team. Why don't you enter for the national championships?"

"The nationals? Are you serious?"

"Why not? I've had to scratch due to conflicting business commitments. I am sure I could arrange for you to take my place."

"That would be great," Galya exclaimed before Frank could respond.

"That's all settled then."

Galya rushed into the flat, bursting to tell Sonia they had won. The flat was empty. There was a note on the table.

I will be out all night.
Hope you had a good day.
Sonia.

Frank saw the look of disappointment on her face. "Never mind," he said, taking her in his arms and hugging her. "You were great to-day, absolutely marvellous." She snuggled up to him.

"I'd rather have your praises than Sonia's," she murmured. I could ask him to stay tonight, she thought. That would be really cosy. Instead, she said, "Frank, do you think you could help me some more?"

"In what way?" he responded letting her go.

Galya went over to the sideboard and got out a bottle of "scotch. "To our future success," she said, handing him a glass in which there was a liberal portion of neat spirit.

Frank laughed. "I know in your country it is customary to drink vodka neat," he said. "In our country we take our whisky with water."

"I do know that," she said going into the kitchen to fetch ice and water. She settled on one end of the couch with her legs tucked under her, Sonia fashion."

"OK, fire away. How can I help?"

"I need some information I can't get hold of. The Trade mission would pay handsomely for your time and effort. I know how difficult it is for you financially at the moment."

"What is this expensive sounding information you are looking for?"

"Airborne infrared surveillance equipment."

Frank gasped. "Galya, you know I can't do that."

"I didn't think you could, but I had to ask."

"Galya, what are you two up to. I thought you were on a buying mission for advanced test equipment that wasn't available in Russia."

"So did I."

"But you are not. What are you up to? It looks to me as though Sonia is running some sort of spy activity and you are part of it. Am I just a pawn in the game? Was our meeting in Brighton really a coincidence?"

Galya looked really miserable. "No - I mean yes it was a coincidence; that is as far as I was concerned. Frank you know I wouldn't play tricks. I asked you for information direct.

I guessed you would refuse. I did need to ask. Oh, Frank, I am so miserable." Tears rolled down her cheeks. The contrast between her earlier happiness and the abject misery now was more than he could stand. He lifted her into his arms, holding her tight until the sobbing stopped. She looked up and he drew her closer, kissing her passionately. "Darling Galya, I love you, I love you."

She released herself and pushed him gently away.

"No Frank, I am leading you into trouble. I love you too. I wouldn't admit it, even to myself, until now. I couldn't bear to hurt you, and yet that is exactly what I am doing. I don't know - I don't know what to do."

"Galya, I want to help you. Be open with me, and I will do what I can to help. Trust me."

"Yes, I will," she whispered putting her finger to her lips, looking with wide eyes at the telephone. Her intuition was right. She hadn't dusted for days, and Sonia never did. The phone wasn't dusty. She threw a cushion over it and led him to the door. "You have stayed too long already," she said.

He looked towards the phone. "Do you think it is bugged?"

"I don't know. I honestly don't know, but I think it might be."

"We must find somewhere to talk."

"Why not the boat? We need to practise for the championships, don't we?"

"If I take tomorrow afternoon off, can you make it?"

"Yes. Where can I meet you? You must not call here again."

"Disappear down the underground. I will meet you at Cockfosters station at one."

She stood on tiptoe and kissed him. "I love you darling, take care."

When Frank had left she took a screwdriver from the kitchen drawer and carefully undid the four screws from the base of the telephone. She lifted the base plate and gazed at the little round disc. It was connected to the outgoing wires by a small circuit board. Clever - they could ring the number and send a coded signal that would inhibit the bell. She carefully screwed the base back.

CHAPTER 7

Galya had a sleepless night. Surely Sonia wasn't eavesdropping on her. The alternative was worse. She would call at Sonia's office, not to tell her about the bug, whoever had planted that was not going learn it had been discovered. She would let Sonia know she was preparing for the national championship races.

As was her normal practice, she knocked on Sonia's door and entered. She stood transfixed. It was not Sonia sitting at the desk. It was a stranger. A man who could loosely be described as middle aged. His dark hair was greying at the sides, giving him a somewhat distinguished appearance. Although he was at the desk Sonia was also in the room, sitting at the corner of the desk, idly swinging her leg back and fro.

"Oh, I am so sorry," began Galya, starting to retreat. "I didn't realise …"

"Don't go," called the stranger. "You must be Galya. We have just been talking about you."

Galya blushed. Sonia smiled at her discomfiture and introduced her to Comrade Lieutenant General Mikhailovitch.

"Good morning Comrade General," stammered Galya.

"Did you enjoy your sailing yesterday," asked the General. More to the point, did you win?"

Galya blushed even more deeply. "We won one," she said.

"Well done. No doubt you will be sailing with Frank Wigmore again."

"Oh, yes," said Galya, wondering how much the General knew of her activities. "That is why I called. The club captain has recommended that we enter the national championships. I agreed to meet Mr Wigmore this afternoon to get in some practice. I thought I should let you know."

The General answered. "Excellent," he said. "Good for our country's improving relations with the people of the United Kingdom. Get all the practice you can. Wouldn't it be great if a combined British-Russian team won?"

"I am afraid we will be outclassed."

"Nonsense. Work at it."

"I will do my best, Comrade General."

"I am sure you will. Off you go."

Sonia raised her eyebrows at the General as Galya closed the door behind her.

"I know what you are thinking," he said, but it is more important now to improve relations with the West. We have had enough spy scandals. I did a lot of thinking whilst in Afghanistan. I would like to see us join the West. The old ways don't work.

"Galya was saying the same thing; co-operation not confrontation."

"Good for her. This is the new thinking in the Kremlin. It doesn't go down too well with the old guard."

"So, we no longer try to compromise Frank Wigmore. I must admit I never thought Galya would co-operate. There will be problems with Comrade Ilyanovitch."

"Yes," mused the General, "there will be problems with Ivan Ilyanovitch. Let's not worry about him." He looked approvingly at Sonia. He used to dream of such a girl in the hell that was Afghanistan, and here she was, and she was his.

Sonia did worry about Ivan Ilyanovitch. One day he would be making one of his routine visits, and this time she was not looking forward to it.

On arriving at his office a little after nine, Frank was asked to report to John Harman's office. John Harman, as Technical Director, was responsible for security and the vetting of technical personnel on behalf of the Ministry of Defence. Frank was not over fond of John Harman. The feeling was mutual.

"Ah, here you are, Frank," John said as Frank entered the office. "I would like you to meet David Blake from the Ministry." He tuned to the man from the Ministry. "David, Frank is Project Leader on the infra red airborne surveillance project, which I am glad to say is going very well; one of the few projects that is actually on time. The trials look very promising."

"Pleased to meet you Frank," said David, rising from his seat to shake hands. Frank responded, not at all pleased to meet him. MI5, no doubt, ex naval officer, spoke with an Oxbridge accent, probably because he was ex-

Oxbridge. Like John Harman he had a slightly supercilious and patronising manner.

"Take a seat, Frank," said John Harman, motioning to a chair on the opposite side of the desk from the man from the Ministry. "We are a little concerned about you."

Frank waited. John Harman looked a bit uncomfortable. Perhaps you had better explain, David," he said.

"We are not at all happy about your close relationship with a member of the Russian Trade Mission. We feel it only fair to warn you that continuing contact would not be wise."

"I don't see why my private life should be any concern of yours."

"You are not that naïve, but obviously you wish me to spell it out. You are in possession of some very sensitive information. Information the Russians would dearly like to have. Your association with a first secretary at the Trade Mission, well versed in the technology is of the greatest concern to us. You should be grateful for a timely word before it is too late."

"Too late?"

"Yes, too late. Only a month or so back a young engineer in a similar position to you compromised himself with an agent from East Germany. We found he was being pressurised to obtain details of the state of the art in secure communications. We prevented him from getting that information. He lost his job. A pity: he was a very good engineer.

"Are you suggesting that I would betray my country?"

"Better people than you have done just that."

"First Secretary Galya Stokowski, for let's not beat about the bush, it is her you are referring to, is not is not an agent. She is a member of a trade delegation openly buying laboratory test equipment that is openly and legitimately available. I have introduced her to sales representatives. Both she and the sales reps are grateful. I have nothing to hide. My association with Galya is quite open, for everyone to see. There is nothing cloak and dagger about it and I resent the suggestion that there is."

"Not at the moment perhaps, but all members of the trade missions are potential agents. They are ideally suited to obtain classified information. That is why we keep tabs on them. I don't believe you have had the opportunity to gather together any information in the short time you have known Galya. What is particularly dangerous in your case is that knowledge could pass verbally and be perfectly understood by your particular contact. At the moment we are giving you the benefit of the doubt, but no longer. Your contact must cease forthwith.

"Rubbish. This is a free country. I can associate with whom I wish so long as I don't break the law of the land, and I have no intention of doing that. Galya is crewing for me in the fireball championships. No doubt she will have told her colleagues at the Embassy by now. If I had to scratch because I would lose my job if I didn't, you, or your political masters, would have to do a bit of explaining to the Russians. I can't imagine they would be too pleased about that. I would take it up with the industrial tribunal and the tabloid press. They would have a field day. In any case I have no intention of disappointing Galya, who is most enthusiastic. I am taking the afternoon off to get some practice. Good day to you."

CHAPTER 8

Midday at Cockfoster's station is a dead time. It is the end of the line, used primarily by commuters for the City and West End. It is situated where suburbia ends and the green belt begins. Thus it was when Galya stepped off the train on what appeared to be a deserted platform. The ticket collector was nowhere to be seen – probably having sandwiches and coffee in his office. Her sandwiches were in her shoulder bag. Some instinct made her put her hand to it. She froze with terror. There was another hand on it. The hand pulled away, but before she could turn round her assailant had an arm round her neck.

Frank, realising he would be early for Galya, stopped at the Cockfoster's shops, half a mile short of the station. He brought two cans of beer to go with the sandwich lunch Galya had insisted on making. He had suggested a pub lunch. Galya had been emphatic that they should have lunch on the island at the sailing club. "I have my reasons," she said. Frank pondered on this as he drove slowly towards the station, slowly until he saw a man with his arm round Galya's neck. He accelerated into the service road and screeched to a halt. To his amazement he saw the man fly over Galya's head and land sprawled out on the pavement. As he opened the door Galya screamed, "NO, get back," and hurled herself into the passenger seat, "Get away from here - fast."

Frank swung the car out of the service road, heading back towards the shopping area, then right into the back roads towards East Barnet and Whetstone where he turned into a supermarket multi-storey car park. He turned towards Galya. She threw herself into his arms and sobbed, shaking. As he caressed her the shaking gradually stopped.

"I'm sorry," she whispered."

"Sorry! You were wonderful."

"Hold me a little longer."

"As long as you like."

After a little while she looked up at him. "Thank you," she said.

"I didn't do anything."

"You were there and now you are here. That was very weak of me to shake like that."

"Weak? Throwing that man. How did you manage it?"

She smiled. "When we were doing our Gymnastic training, we used to practise the martial arts for fun. There's quite a knack in throwing someone nearly twice your weight."

"You are the most fantastic person I have ever met. We should have called the police."

"No. That would have meant getting the Russian Embassy involved with all the ramifications that would create."

"True. In the meantime, you need a hot sweet drink. You have had a shock."

"I have a flask of coffee in my shoulder bag. If it was money our friend was after he would have been disappointed."

"You think it was a mugging?"

Galya thoughtfully unscrewed the top of the thermos flask, poured out some coffee, took a sip and passed it to Frank. "I think it must have been. Nothing else makes sense. If someone was trying to obtain incriminating evidence they would have waited till after we had met: assuming they knew."

"My lot know. I was warned off you first thing this morning. I told them I was going to meet you - and why."

"I am sorry Frank. I don't want to get you into trouble. Did you tell them I had asked for classified information?"

"No. I know you didn't want to ask, so I kept quiet about it. Are you being pressurised for it?"

"Not at the moment. I told Sonia that you were not the sort of person that would pass classified information, and I was not the sort of person to ask for it. She has accepted that for now."

"Some of the technical journals go into surprising detail about the work you are interested in. I will look some out for you. It might satisfy your people without betraying any confidences.

"Frank, you are being very good to me. I do appreciate it. Please don't prejudice your position."

"I won't. We are sailing partners. I have told my people. I think it would be wise to show up at the club."

"Too right. Let's go."

Galya remained quiet during the journey. As they pulled into the club car park, she suggested they parked among the trees near the lake. "I'll explain later," she said. She got out and felt with her hands under each of the wheel arches. Then lying on her back, despite Frank's protests, she wormed her way under the rear of the car. "I thought as much," she said, pulling away a small metal box that had been magnetically attached to the petrol tank. "Someone is interested in your whereabouts, or to be more precise, our whereabouts."

"Let me have that," said Frank. I'll chuck it in the lake."

"As we are exactly where we said we would be it might be wiser to put it back; then they, whoever they are will not know that we know."

"Who do you think they are?"

"I can't see what interest my people would have in your whereabouts, with or without me. However the bug on the telephone could not have been your people."

"How do you work that out?"

"They would have heard me ask for classified information, thrown the book at you, and advised the trade mission I was no longer welcome in this country. I would be packing my bags by now."

"So, we are both under surveillance from both sides."

CHAPTER 9

Comrade Ivan Ilyanovitch was not a happy man. Glasnost and perestroika were not to his liking. He was a KGB man. In the Russia he knew the KGB were all-powerful. They were Gods: Gods to be feared. No longer. There were phone-ins to the nice KGB.

The work with the Trade Missions was only part of his activity. He had agents all over Europe. Apart from active agents there were sleeping agents, waiting to act when the time was right, creating unrest, subversion, and instability, to take over if the government could be toppled.

Perestroika may be the buzzword at the moment, but who had the power to dismantle the KGB with all its ramifications. A few months ago Comrade Ilyanovitch would have said no one; but things were changing at the top. A regular army man who had made a name for himself by successfully extricating his troops from one of the most difficult situations in Afghanistan had been promoted to General and put in charge of Directorate T which covered the European operations. A hero for retreating! The General's mission at the KGB was to promote a less belligerent image. There were those in the KGB who had no intention of retreating. The General and his liberal minded masters would have to go.

In the meantime Ilyanovitch had two reports in front of him to consider. A meticulous report from First Secretary Galya Stokowski outlined the complete purchasing package required to bring the research labs up to date. A second report was from Sonia Medov. Had he allowed his emotions to override his judgement? She was put in place to do as instructed - not to have opinions. Galya had made a very useful contact. Information on airborne infrared surveillance equipment was urgent. If Galya didn't know how to go about it he would instruct her. He would enjoy that. The thought gave some satisfaction. He would make a visit to London.

Sonia confided to Galya that she was in love for the first time in her life and was afraid for the first time in her life. She dreaded a visit from Ivan. Any agent suspected of playing false was never the same again after interrogation by him, if indeed they were ever seen again.

Ivan Ilyanovitch felt better as soon as he boarded the Aeroflot Ilyushin 62. He recalled they served scotch in the VIP class. He ordered a double. He thought of Sonia and felt considerably better. He should have let her know he was coming. Never mind, she would know soon enough. He ordered a bottle of wine with his lunch and a brandy with his coffee. Hard drinker that he was, he realised he had overdone it on the flight. After clearing customs at Heathrow he took a taxi to the flat. A change and freshen up was called for.

Sonia and the General lingered over lunch. "You tempt me to stay on in London," said the General" but I must leave tomorrow."

"I'll miss you. Where are you going next?"

"Paris."

"Lucky you."

"Would you like to come? I need an assistant who understands the language."

"Do you have to ask? What of my work here?"

"Your work doesn't have the same priority now. We are looking forward to a new era."

"Co-operation not confrontation. I would like to move to the diplomatic staff and play a part in the new international scene."

"Then stay close to me. With your experience and fluency in both French and English there should be no problem."

"Leo darling, you are wonderful."

"Then join me at my hotel tonight and I will tell you how wonderful you are."

"OK. I'll pick up a few things and leave a note for my flat mate. Poor Galya. She would love to ask Frank to stay, but is determined not to get him into trouble, and I no longer care, thanks to you."

Sonia heard movements upstairs as she entered the flat. "Hi, Galya," she called, "You are back early."

"Hello, Shonia darling," slurred Ilyanovitch. "No need to go to the office now. There are better things to do."

"Ivan, you surprised me. No, not now, I have a headache. That is why I am back early. I really don't feel very well."

"You look well enough to me." He leered at her. He picked up the bottle of scotch already half empty and poured a liberal portion into the empty glass on the table. He lifted the glass, paused, and offered it to Sonia. "You had better have a drink - do you good."

"No thank you Ivan; and don't you think you have had enough."

His eyes blazed with anger, as he moved menacingly towards her "Don't tell me what to do and not to do." She backed away and fell backwards onto the settee. He was on her before she could escape, tearing desperately at her blouse. A few months previously she would have yielded and let him have his way until his passion was spent. Now she turned her face away and buried it into the settee. He stepped back, black fury in his face. What's wrong with you? Why don't you respond?"

"She looked up to him, petrified at what she saw. "I don't feel well", she whimpered. This time it was true.

"So you are not feeling well. Let us talk then, for that was the prime reason for my visit. And, believe me, if you are not feeling well now, you will be feeling much worse when we have finished."

"Can't it wait? I really have had a difficult day."

"Will you stop telling me what to do. I put you here and I expect you to do as you are told - without question. Is that understood?"

"Yes Ivan."

"Then why haven't you got that clever little friend of yours to get on the job with Wigmore."

"She is not that sort of person."

"Then it is about time she was. She has to earn her keep the same as you."

"She wasn't sent here for espionage. You said yourself we needed expertise. We have others for that sort of work."

He eyed her intently. "I decide who does what sort of work. Galya is going to learn a new trade and I am going to teach her."

"You bastard."

This time she did not back away quickly enough and he caught her a resounding blow to the side of her face that sent her crashing to the floor.

"Get up," he sneered. "I haven't finished with you yet." She stayed whimpering on the floor. "Get up, I said." Slowly she got to her feet and backed away from him. He backed her into a corner, grabbed her hair, pulling her head back forcing her to look into his face contorted with rage and hatred. "Nobody, but nobody calls me a bastard. If it weren't for the fact that you have to go through a foreign airport I would smash your face to pulp. "Now get back to your office, clear your desk and book an immediate flight back to Moscow. Pack a few things and get out of this flat. I have other business here."

Sonia flew up to her room, grateful to be out of his way. She threw a few essential items into her case, anxious only to get out of the building as soon as possible. She reached the door without being molested further. Making her way back to the trade mission she had no recollection of the streets or the traffic.

If anyone at the trade mission noticed an uncharacteristically dishevelled head of department rush headlong into her office they made no comment. She slammed the door behind her and grabbed the phone. It was not the Aeroflot booking office she was ringing. It was the General's number at the Embassy. His secretary answered. The General was not in the office. She thought he mentioned something about having a haircut before returning to his hotel. Sonia stared in horror and disbelief at the phone. Would Galya be raped because General Mikailovitch was having a haircut?

"Can I leave a message, Comrade Medov?" enquired the voice on the phone.

"Yes. Tell him I want to speak to him urgently. Are you expecting him back before he returns to his hotel?

"He has some documents and letters to sign, so he may be back later."

"I will come to his office.

CHAPTER 10

"Shall I take you back to your flat?" enquired Frank

"No, you can drop me off at any station on the Piccadilly Line except Cockfosters."

"Are you sure, after your earlier experience?"

"That's not likely to happen again. All the stations will be busy now with returning commuters. There is no point in aggravating your domestic problems further."

"Southgate is in the middle of a busy shopping area. I'll drop you there." He stopped outside the station. "Take care," he said leaning across to kiss her. He watched her go into the station and was about to drive off when the passenger door opened.

"May I come in," said David Blake, doing just that.

"Be my guest."

"Thank you. You had better drive off. You are on a double yellow line." Frank pulled away from the kerb.

"Do you want a lift back to the firm? I have to call back to sign a couple of letters."

"No need. Pull in round the corner." Frank complied.

"Very touching scene at the station," said David Blake.

"You must be very proud of yourself, playing Peeping Tom."

"It's a little bit more serious than that. Why aren't you taking our advice? You could easily extricate yourself from the sailing championships."

"I could, but I won't. I have never had such a good crew. I've told my wife and she is pleased that I have found a regular crew and won't be encouraging my daughters to sail anymore."

"You are avoiding the issue. I made further enquiries into your past projects and was horrified to find that prior to your present work you were involved with secure radio communications. In particular implementing the codes for fast channel changing to make it impossible for a third party to eavesdrop unless they knew how the sequence was selected. You are one of the few people who could tell them."

"I am well aware of the sensitivity of that information. I have no intention of discussing it with anyone."

"Now we are getting to the basic problem. You find that information a burden, don't you?"

"Not until you came along."

"Are you telling me that consorting with an agent from the one country that would be most interested in that knowledge doesn't worry you?"

"As I saw it the security aspect was in your hands. Nobody was supposed to know I was working on that project. I never mentioned it to anyone, not even my wife. If there was a security leak it must have been in your department. Judging from past history that would not surprise me. In my younger days I used to believe that all our guys were like

"Bulldog" Drummond or Richard Hannay, or even 007. How disillusioned can you get?"

"All the more reason to take care in the real world."

"I am"

"You are in danger."

"Who from?"

"From yourself. You are deliberately putting your self under emotional strain, both at work and in your private life. We have been worried about the number of engineers working in a similar environment to yourself who have committed suicide in recent years. You must have seen the reports in the press."

"I certainly have. Suicide for no apparent reason. The one thing they had in common was that they were working on top-secret projects and were privy to sensitive information. The official view was that the pressure got them down. Yet in every case family, friends and colleagues agreed that they were perfectly happy."

"I wouldn't like to see you go that way."

"Is that a warning, a threat or both?"

"Now you are being dramatic."

"Am I? I have given a lot of thought to those suicides. I have worked on Defence projects throughout my career. I have never found it stressful. On the contrary, defence work is invariably interesting and absorbing, often ahead of the state of the art. It is more akin to academic research. It is working in the commercial competitive market with management leaning on you that is stressful. Ministry of Defence work is much more laid back.   In peace it is only the government auditors that get upset.   There is something distinctly fishy about those suicides.   If you want to safeguard secrets, what better way than eliminate those in possession of them?"

"You have been reading too many spy novels. Getting back to reality, don't you think it would be better for you to stop seeing your Russian friend before it ruins your marriage."

"My marriage is only a token affair now for the sake of the children. I could dwell on it and get morbid. My friendship with Galya is an antidote to that. It's no strain. It is a pleasure."

"So, what do you talk about when you are together, apart from sailing?"

"It is easier to tell you what we don't talk about.   We do not discuss the confidential details of my work.   We do agree on the stupidity of the East-West divide.   Is that subversive?"

"In our book it is the thin edge of the wedge, softening you up to talk a little more uninhibitedly about your work."

"Our work is the last thing we want to talk about when we are together."

"So you are off your guard. All part of the strategy."

"I tell you Galya is not a spy."

"Her boss is."

"You mean Sonia Medov?"

"No, although the French suspected her of clandestine activities when she was stationed in Paris. It is the overall controller, a certain Ivan Ilyanovitch. He is known to be high up in the KGB and to control a spy network. We learned he is coming over today under the guise of superintendent of the Soviet Trade Mission. Furthermore he has given as his London address the flat in St Johns Wood where your friend lives. He has stayed there before. So he and your friend Galya will soon be having a cosy little chat."

Frank was silent. If the MI5 man's statement was true then Galya was embroiled in a spy network. Knowing that the flat was bugged she would be careful not to incriminate either of them - or would she? It could be an MI5 bug. Blake would know, but would he admit it?

"So you will find out if I have given anything away. You will have the flat bugged, no doubt."

"Of course not. The last thing we would wish is the discovery of a bugging device in a private residence. Imagine the reaction, not only in Moscow, but here as well."

"You had no such inhibitions fitting a transmitting device to my car."

"That is very different. It doesn't involve another country."

"So you admit it."

"Why deny it when you already know. If you knew it was there why didn't you remove it?"

"Why should I? I have nothing to hide and it was more interesting finding out who was checking up on me. It was obvious when you turned up dead on cue at the station."

David Blake fished out a pipe from his pocket. He slowly and deliberately filled it.

"Mind if I smoke? He asked, pausing with a match at the ready."

"Looks like a fait accompli." Frank eyed the heavy black bowl of the pipe. "Perhaps you could open your window a shade. It looks as if that monster needs a chimney."

David Blake got the pipe going to his satisfaction and stared at nothing in particular through the windscreen." "I am inclined to think you are clean," he said.

"Thanks a lot."

David Blake ignored the remark. "I would like your help," he said. Frank waited. David Blake pushed the tobacco more firmly into the bowl of his pipe. We have an interest in Ivan Ilyanovitch. He waltzes around Europe organising his spy network with immunity. We need to discover his modus operandi."

"I don't see how I can help do that. If you think I am going to involve Galya in counter espionage, think again."

"You are jumping to conclusions. If what you say is correct, and I have no reason to believe it isn't, then Galya has not been involved in any covert operations. However Ilyanovitch is bound to learn of her contact. He will make investigations. He will probably discover that you were working on secure communications, simply by where you were working and when. Then it will be interesting to see what move he makes. We would like you to tell us."

"You want me to spy for you."

"No, only to report if you are asked to betray your country."

“I would do that anyway.”

“Even if it meant reporting Galya?”

“That is irrelevant. She would not involve herself in such activities.”

“So you will help us.”

“I will report if anyone asks me to betray my country.”

“Good. Happy sailing.”

CHAPTER 11

General Mikhailovitch, assessing the European activities of the KGB, felt it necessary to stand back from the everyday details to take a detached and objective view of the operation. With this in mind he had deliberately taken the afternoon off to have a much-needed haircut, followed by a walk through the parks, hoping to pick up some of the atmosphere of the country. He was fascinated with Britain. He had studied its military history whilst at the Military Academy. Pausing at Buckingham Palace to watch the changing of the guard he realised he was rubbing shoulders with every nationality but the British. It was time he got back to the office.

His secretary gave him the reports she had been typing for his approval and signature. She seemed ill at ease.

"Is something wrong, Natalia?" he asked.

She hesitated.

"What is it?" he persisted.

"I thought you should know that Comrade Medov was here earlier. She said she needed to see you urgently."

"So why didn't she wait for me?"

"I think she thought you would go straight to your hotel."

The General frowned. What could be so urgent that it could not have waited to this evening? "Call her office and see if she is there."

"I "phoned as soon as you came in. I was told she had not been back since she left to come here."

"What about her flat?"

"I "phoned there too."

"And?"

"A man answered the "phone."

"Oh, did he say who he was?"

No, Comrade General. He just said she was no longer there and put down the phone. She hesitated again. "I thought he sounded like Comrade Ilyanovitch," she said.

"He should have informed me if he was coming to England."

"There is a copy of a signal in your IN tray that relates to a visit to London prior to meeting you in Paris. You may recall Comrade General that you changed your schedule. You were due in Paris today."

The General did not reply.

"Excuse me, Comrade General."

"Yes?"

"I thought Comrade Medov might have been in an accident."

"An accident? What do you mean?"

"Comrade Medov looked very distressed and had a bruise under her left eye."

Comrade General Mikhailovitch left the office without signing his reports and letters.

Galya was not happy going back to the flat. Sonia would not be there and it would be empty and lonely. Why did Frank leave her to go home alone? It had been her idea, but that did not stop the resentment. It was with a heavy heat and a sense of foreboding that she entered the flat. It smelt of cigarette smoke. Neither she nor Sonia smoked.

"That must be Galya," called a vaguely familiar voice. "Come up, my dear." She felt like turning and running away, but continued up the stairs.

Ivan Ilyanovitch was sitting at the table sipping black coffee and studying the file he had in front of him.

"So we meet again, my dear," he said.

"Good evening, Comrade. I was not expecting to find you here."

"An unexpected pleasure for you. I bring greetings from your mother. She seems to be enjoying her stay in the sanatorium.

"I am glad to hear it Comrade."

Thanks to you, my dear, she is a privileged person. I trust it will stay that way."

"I hope so too."

"Then you must do a little more for us. Sit down, my dear. Would you like some of this excellent coffee, or something a little stronger, perhaps?"

"I would appreciate the coffee. Thank you."

"You look cold. I will add a drop of whisky" This he did before she could protest. Nonetheless it was welcome and warming.

"As I was saying," he continued. "We were pleased to get the transputer and all the associated data. I imagine that as with all the other equipment you were able to obtain it over the counter for cash."

Of course. It was freely available. That is what I am here to do."

"No, you are here to do a little more than that." He paused. Galya made no response. Do you know what I mean?" he persisted.

"No, Comrade," she lied.

"You have a relationship with a very knowledgeable engineer, yet you have given us nothing of his work. That is not good enough."

"My relationship is purely as crew for his boat. He has helped me with contacts for obtaining advanced measuring equipment."

"That is nothing. You have obtained no information relating to infrared airborne surveillance equipment. He is an authority on that."

"He is not permitted to discuss it."

"You could persuade him."

"No, comrade, I could not."

"You could and I am going to show you how."

"To pressurise him would ruin our friendship."

"I did not say pressurise. I said persuade. I will show you how to make him want to give it to you. I taught Sonia. She enjoyed it, and so did I. Now I will teach you. This will be even more intriguing." He came and stood at the back of his chair and laid his hands gently on her shoulders. She froze. He slid his hands to her breasts. "Come", he said, "we will do better in Sonia's room."

"Sonia will be back soon," said Galya in desperation."

"No Sonia will not be back. I have sent her away. We have the flat to ourselves."

"I am not staying here without Sonia," gasped Galya, rushing for the door.

Ivan had anticipated this and stood between her and the door. "You are mistaken," he smiled. You are staying here with me." Galya stared at him with horror. "Sit down again, Galya, and calm down. You and I are going to have another little talk." Realising she had no option Galya sat down again. Ivan Ilyanovitch sat down beside her, on the door side. "Listen carefully," he said. "The continuation of your position and your mother's special treatment is up to me, and only me. Do you understand?"

"I didn't ask for this position and in particular to be an agent."

"Your duties are decided by me."

Galya eyed the phone and wondered if there was friend or foe at the other end. "I respect your authority, Comrade Ilyanovitch, she said. That does not mean I have to prostitute myself at your command."

"You take after your father. Oh, yes, I know all about him. He refused to toe the party line. He was lucky. If he had not have been terminally ill he would have been sent to Siberia."

"My father was an honest man and of the highest principles," bristled Galya. He was a firm supporter of communism. He would have nothing to do with the brutality of Stalinism. Time has vindicated his ideals. Ideals I share and hope to see fulfilled."

"Don't lecture me. Stalin set up the KGB. It held Russia together in the past, and it is the only hope of holding it together in the future. I represent the KGB. The KGB is strong. We are the masters. I am your master, and you will do as I say - now. As he got up and came towards her she jumped up, and swerved round him making for the door. He flung himself at her, knocking her to the floor, falling on top of her. She lay face down panting for breath. He grasped her free arm, twisting it to force her round to face him. He leered down at her. "No, my girl," he said, "you don't get away from me that easily. Now are you going to come with me quietly like a sensible girl?

"No, never," she gasped.

He gave her arm a sharp twist. She screamed with pain. Instinctively he put his hand over her mouth. Galya opened her mouth and caught his little finger in her teeth. She bit hard. It was his turn to cry out in pain, relaxing his grip. She turned and sharply arched her back, jerking herself from under him as he fell to one side against the door. She vaulted over the table, turned and faced him as he slowly got to his feet. "You little cat," he snarled. "I'll punish you for this."

He pushed the table to the side, upsetting the Whisky bottle, cups and glasses. He moved menacingly towards her intent on backing her into the corner. She did not move back. Perplexed, he paused. Galya's left leg shot out hitting him in the abdomen. As he doubled up in pain Galya swung both fists together hard into his face. His head jerked back with blood pouring from his nose.

Sonia and the General, having met at the hotel were in the surveillance room at the Embassy. General Mikhailovitch ordered the surveillance line to the flat to be activated. Sonia raised her eyebrows. "Yes, I ordered the surveillance," he said. "I thought Galya might be planning to defect to live with Frank Wigmore."

Sonia had no chance to reply. The technician had switched the phone bug response to the loudspeakers. There was a massive crash and sound of breaking glass. The General rapped out an order for his car and personal chauffeur.

"With all this traffic we would have done better on foot," complained Sonia when they were in the car.

"Possibly," replied the General, "but we might need my chauffeur." He nodded to the thickset driver.

Sonia wasted no time in unlocking the flat. It was silent. All three rushed up the stairs. Sonia flung open the door of the living room. They all stopped dead. Kneeling on the floor amongst the broken glass and ornaments was Galya quietly wiping away the blood from Ivan Ilyanovitch's gashed face while he lay on his back on the sofa, holding an ice bag over his forehead and nose. "I am afraid Comrade Ilyanovitch has had a slight accident," Galya said, as she calmly applied another Band-Aid across one of the many cuts on his face.

"I am of the opinion that that is a slight understatement, young lady," said the General. "When you have finished patching up Comrade

Ilyanovitch I think a little talk is called for. You may wait in the car, Leon."

"Very good, Comrade General," replied his chauffeur.

"And Leon," added the General as the chauffeur was leaving, "you have seen nothing tonight."

"I understand, Comrade General."

CHAPTER 12

Ivan Ilyanovitch 'and General Mikhailovitch faced one another across the table. Sonia and Galya had cleared most of the mess and General Mikhailovitch had ordered them to get hotel accommodation for the night, forbidding Ilyanovitch to leave the flat. "I am not going to have you seen in that condition," he had stated.

Ivan Ilyanovitch was on the defensive, responding to his embarrassing situation by adopting an excessively deferential attitude bordering on the insolent. The General knew he had to tread carefully. He was a new boy at the top and an outsider. He was well aware that Ivan Ilyanovitch and his associates who had been passed over would miss no opportunity to discredit him. The curbing of some of the more outrageous activities of the KGB was unpopular among the die-hards as was the withdrawal from Afghanistan among the old guard of the army. Dissatisfaction among senior army officers could be dangerous to the regime and the support of the secret police was essential.

"You need the information my European organisation supplies," Ivan Ilyanovitch was saying. "It is not only industrial know-how we obtain, but important military data."

"The military espionage is not now of such importance that we risk damaging our relations with the West with such activities. The priorities have changed."

"You do not need me to tell you, Comrade General that as a military strategist it is essential to know what your potential adversary is thinking, in peace as much as in war. How else can you negotiate in confidence?"

"That is true," agreed the General.

"And aren't you in difficulties with the new frequency hopping techniques now being introduced into NATO radio communications."

The General looked up at him. "Yes we are. It is no longer sufficient to be able to unscramble or correct the code if it is not possible to stay on the channel long enough to process the data before the channel changes.

Exactly, and to follow the channel changes you need to know the channel changing programme. Did you know that Frank Wigmore worked on channel changing techniques and undoubtedly holds information that could be of great assistance to us?"

"How did you know he had worked on that project?" enquired the General, his interest aroused.

"I do my homework," said Ivan Ilyanovitch, smugly.

"We will have to review the situation. Perhaps Galya could lure him to Russia."

"He would be dissuaded from leaving with such sensitive information."

"True, I would guess he is already being watched. MI5 will have been alerted to his association with Galya."

Undoubtedly. They would have been keeping an eye on the staff at the Trade

Mission. They have scared or warned off one or two useful contacts recently."

They don't appear to have warned off Frank Wigmore. He was sailing with Galya this afternoon. They are entering for the class championships; a practical example of friendly co-operation between the two countries. I would not wish to jeopardise it with the risk of yet another spy scandal. We should keep Galya clean. The thawing of East-West relations has to be balanced against the need to know."

The General got out his pipe and filled it with care. He lit it and leaned back in his chair apparently engrossed in getting it to draw to his complete satisfaction. "Perhaps," he said, we can manage an East-West co-operative venture and the acquisition of knowledge as a bonus. Leave Galya to me. I would think you would be glad to see the back of her."

On the contrary, she has all the qualities I prize. They should be harnessed to the cause of our great revolution."

"They will be harnessed for the good of Russia."

"What of Comrade Medov. Her work has been unsatisfactory recently and you cannot believe a word she says I am replacing her and have ordered her back to headquarters."

The General looked long and hard at the man opposite. "It is not Comrade Medov who is returning to Moscow. It is you. I will arrange leave for you until your face has a chance to look a little more respectable. As for Comrade Medov, I will arrange for a transfer to the diplomatic corps. With fluency in French and German, together with a good working knowledge of English, that should be no problem."

"Ivan Ilyanovitch scowled "What of the Paris operations review. You know nothing of the network I have established in France."

"Our man in Paris will have sufficient knowledge to enable me to close down our covert operations there. We will keep sufficient sleepers there in case of a change.

"You will regret it."

"We shall see." The General stood up and prepared to leave. As he went to the door he turned. "When you get back to Moscow you will not leave Russia again without my permission. Is that clear?"

"Yes, Comrade General."

The chauffeur opened the rear door for the General. As the car drew away from the flat the General asked: "did you arrange accommodation for the girls, Leon?"

"There was a spare room at the staff flat for Galya. I took Comrade Medov to your hotel."

"Drive to the hotel then."

Leon smiled. "Better than Afghanistan, Comrade General."

"You can say that again, Sergeant."

CHAPTER 13

"So you are an expert on frequency agile communications." Galya gave Frank a mischievous half smile. They were finishing their picnic lunch on the island in the middle of the sailing club lake. They had been training for the fireball championships for the last month now, taking time off during the week when the club was deserted. They could relax and talk freely on the island. A swan's nest on the side of the island nearest the clubhouse would give a noisy warning of the approach of any other intruders. Their relationship and mutual trust had matured, as had their sailing competence. It was now accepted at the club that they would be among the race leaders and often the outright winners.

"No one is supposed to know that. Are you being pressurised again?"

"Not so much pressurised as persuaded by Sonia's boss's boss; and I'll not tell you who he is then you will not have anything you feel you should tell your man. He seems to be leaving you alone now."

"He is hoping we will get married. Then, as a British citizen you could advise us of the hierarchy that controls you."

Galya laughed. "They want me to persuade you to defect to us. They badly need that information on channel hopping communications. Aren't I seductive enough to persuade you?"

"We are playing a dangerous game. You know I would marry you because I love you. Why don't you want to live over here?"

"Why should I? I love my country, despite its politics, and that is where I want to live. I can't imagine living anywhere else. Why is it that the wife has to live in the country of the husband?

"I would be in control if we stayed in this country. I could look after you and help you. In Russia you would be in control."

"You are a male chauvinist pig. I would help you adapt in Russia, just as you would look after me here."

Frank was silent. He knew it wouldn't work in Russia.

"It's time we got in some sailing practice," Galya said. "Are you going to let me helm next Sunday?"

"You had us disqualified from the last race, not giving way to a boat on starboard tack."

"We were rounding the mark. We were entitled to clear water, whether or not we were on port tack."

"That wasn't the committee's view."

"That was because it was the honorary Commodore's son who made the protest."

"I was surprised at the decision. We'll have another look at the rulebook. It might be worth appealing. In the meantime you can helm for both races to make up for it."

"I could win if I had a better crew."

"I've changed my mind. You can only helm for one race."

"Beast."

"Galya, keep your head down. There is someone in the car park."

They peered through the thick bushes hiding them from anyone at or near the clubhouse. Frank sensed danger. Had he made a mistake in choosing such a lonely place to meet? It was a good place to talk. He remembered the engineers who had died in mysterious circumstances. In such a place as this anything could happen - an accidental capsize - knocked unconscious by the boom - trapped under the hull and drowned. He knew he should not have been sailing without rescue facilities available. Galya sensed his concern and squeezed his hand.

"What do you think he is doing here?" she whispered.

"I wish I knew. He hasn't come to sail, wearing collar and tie and military style mackintosh. He's not here to sell insurance. He looks more like the man from the Mafia. I can't see well enough to be sure, but he doesn't look like a club member. I would recognise most of the members. So he is trespassing on private ground. He's bad news."

"Should we wait and see if he goes away?"

"Not much point. He knows we are here. He will have seen our car, and if he takes a walk round the lake, as he has just started doing, he will see us. Let's get going and take the initiative. They launched the fireball back into the water and hoisted the sails. "We'll go round the other side, where we will be out of his view, until we are opposite the jetty; then we'll make a dash for it. I'll feel happier on terra firma. We are two and we are forewarned."

They tacked round the opposite side of the island, Frank estimating the pace of the walker. When they had clear water between themselves and the jetty they had the wind abeam and made straight for it, turning into wind at the last moment to come to a stop alongside. They jumped ashore and secured the boat as the big man approached.

Galya squeezed Frank's hand. "Don" worry," she said. "I recognise him. Let me do the talking."

"Well met, Comrade Leon," she said, speaking in Russian. "You are the last person I expected to see."

"Well met indeed Comrade. You were not intended to see me. I was anxious when I did not see your boat, knowing you were here."

"Why am I under observation? Was it to see that I did not defect?"

"It was not you I was observing. It is the safety of your friend that concerns the General.

"I don't understand."

"It seems he has sensitive information. Other engineers in the defence industry have - and I quote - committed suicide. Dead men tell no tales. The General is anxious that this should not happen to your friend. He hopes you will be able to extract that information eventually."

Galya bit her lip. She recalled the long talk she had had with the General. He had been most emphatic about the importance of the information required on the programming of frequency agile communications. She had seen how important it was for the policies of Russia to know what the West was thinking, especially when there was a tendency to trust the West as they had never trusted them before. It was necessary to keep your guard up. She had promised to do all she could without causing a rift with Frank. She was, and always would be a loyal citizen of Russia.

Frank, seeing her concern, asked what it was all about.

"You are in danger, Frank. I will tell you on the way home."

Leon said, in passable English: "It would be advisable not to come here any more alone."

"Is it true," said Galya, as they were returning in the car, "that several engineers working in your defence industry have committed suicide for no apparent reason?"

"Yes. There never has been a satisfactory explanation."

"The break up of your marriage and your financial worries would give a very plausible reason for your suicide. Are your people really capable of that sort of thing?

"Until a few years ago I would have said no, it is only your KGB that would carry out that sort of activity. Now I am not so sure."

"It is my understanding that an assassination by the KGB needs the authority of the head of the First Directorate at least, and he has to be given a very convincing argument for it. In your country the only criterion is that they must not be found out."

"You seem very knowledgeable on the subject."

"You can read it all in your local library."

The following morning Frank went straight to John Harman's office. "How do I get in touch with David Blake?" he asked.

"Easy, it just so happens he wants to see you. He is already here. You will find him waiting for you in your office." Frank left John's office without a further word. He found David Blake sitting at his desk making a "phone call.

"Ah, here you are," he said putting down the phone. "Take a seat."

"Thank you, and you are welcome to use my desk."

"There is no need for that attitude. You are in no position to be cocky. What the hell are you playing at? It's bad enough carrying on with that Russian girl. Now you seem buddies with the KGB. This is something altogether different."

"I know nothing of the KGB. If you are referring to the guy who turned up at the sailing club yesterday, I know nothing about him. He spoke to Galya in Russian. I think he was concerned that she was going to defect. In which case he was more right than he realised. I would love to be able to persuade her to stay. Not that she would be any use to you. She is no more likely to betray her country than I am, and she is not party to any confidential information. But that is not what I came to see you about,"

"Haven't you got it the wrong way round. I came to see you.

"No, I have not got it the wrong way round. I have something to tell you."

"I'm listening."

"The first thing you should know is that I have written to the editors of all the Yachting magazines to advise them that I am entering the fireball championships with a Russian crew. I have also written a letter to my solicitor saying that if I met with an accident or appear to have committed suicide he is to initiate and pursue enquiries into the circumstances, however plausible they appear.

"I can see it is useless talking to you. You are fantasising."

"In that case get out of my office. I have work to do and want no part of your silly spy games. If you want to waste taxpayers money having me followed that is your business. I have nothing to hide."

"You do have something to hide - information."

"Get stuffed."

CHAPTER 14

Alexei was frowning at the letter he had received from Galya. He was spending the weekend with his parents at their Dacha.

"What's worrying you? asked his father, who had been pleased to see how his son had settled down to a much quieter lifestyle in recent months, spending more time at the Dacha at weekends, relaxing from new and more onerous responsibilities. The political uncertainty and upheaval of recent times was felt more acutely in the world of banking than in Dr. Bronowski's academic world.

"I have been reading Galya's last letter."

"How is she getting on?"

She seems to be having a wonderful time."

"So what's worrying you? You should be relieved. She was not at all happy about going."

"She is happy enough now. I miss her. I wish she was back. I feel she is slipping away from me."

"You didn't seem to worry a damn while she was here."

"I let her know how I felt before she left."

"What did she say?"

"Nothing much. She gave an enigmatic smile and said she would soon be back. I wonder if she will come back, and if she does will she be the same?"

"Not exactly the same. Like you she will have moved on in life. Her nature and character won't change. Why do you wonder if she will come back?"

"She has met an Englishman who was over here for a symposium some years ago. She was his translator. They go sailing together. She is going to crew for him in the British championships and perhaps the international championships. How can I compete with that?"

"By being Russian. She is unlikely to be affected by the prosperity of the West. She is Russian, and it is in Russia she will want to live."

"I wish I could share you confidence."

Dr. Bronowski was not as confident as he sounded. Unknown to his son, he had been summoned to report to the headquarters of the First Chief Directorate of the KGB in Yasenov, on the outskirts of Moscow. There was nothing unusual in this. His advice was often sought by the Directorate of Intelligence and Information (Analysis and Assessment). This request however had come from Directorate T - Active Measures.

The summons came soon after a surprise visit from the new Deputy Director, a General, who had been seconded from the army. He had come to let Dr. Bronowski know that he had met and talked to Galya in London. She was concerned for her mother, not for her health, which had been improving at the sanatorium, but for her safety. The General had suggested that Dr and Mrs Bronowski might take her into their household. His prestige and standing in the party should then ensure that she was not got at to pressurise Galya in any way. The

General would not be more specific, except to say Galya was a credit to her country.

The summons to Yasanov, Dr. Bronowski feared had something to do with Galya.

His fears were not without foundation. Arriving the following week at the prestigious headquarters, he was kept waiting outside the Deputy Directors office on the second floor of the right wing of the massive 22 story building. He had the feeling that inside this building there was a world that was remote and different to the real world outside. The people in occupation were powerful and privileged. They had risen above their fellow countrymen and cut off from the rank and file members of the party. They had their own apartment blocks, access to special clinics and hospitals, and their exclusive Dzerzhinsky club. In the soviet state concluded Dr Bronowski there were rulers and ruled. There was a great gulf between them and the rulers intended that it should stay that way.

Deep in his reverie he hardly noticed the door of the Deputy Director's office open. "Please come in, Comrade Doctor," invited the poker-faced apparatchik, standing aside for him.

On entering, he noticed there were six others sitting round a baize-covered table. Each position had a notepad, tumbler and carafe of water. He recognised only two of those present - Colonel Ilyanovitch, and Lieutenant General Mikhailovitch. General Mikhailovitch was the only one to acknowledge his presence. "Welcome Comrade Doctor," he said. "We are about to come to your area of interest." He motioned to a spare place at the opposite end of the table; a position from where Dr. Bronowski could study the grim impassive features of the other members of the committee seated at each side of the table

Without further preamble the General asked, "What do you know of frequency agile communications, Dr. Bronowski?"

"We are working on such a system in my department, Comrade General, responded Dr Bronowski. "It is a method of tactical radio communication whereby the transmitter and receiver hop simultaneously from one frequency to another at programmed intervals, thus preventing any third party that does not have access to the programme from holding onto the transmission long enough to make any sense out of it. This is an advance on sending messages in code, enabling a third party to decode or unscramble the message. With the system we have produced it is impossible for anyone other than the intended recipient to keep a hold on the transmission."

"Absolutely impossible?" queried the General.

"What if a third party got hold of the programme," interjected Colonel Ilyanovitch.

"Then they would be in the same position as the intended recipient."

"So it is not impossible for a third party to intercept the message," persisted Colonel Ilyanovitch, giving the General a meaningful look.

"It is impossible without the programme is what I meant," said Dr Bronowski, who thought this was perfectly obvious. What were they getting at?

"Would Comrade Galya Stokowski be able to understand the system?"

So that was it. Danger bells rang in Dr. Bronowski's head. "She has never worked on it," he said.

"What we asked," said Colonel Ilyanovitch, who seemed to have taken over the meeting, "was would she be able to understand the system, yes or no."

"Yes."

"That confirms our belief." The others round the table, except the General, nodded solemnly. "You have the solution to your intelligence problem, Comrade General."

"Perhaps. Dr. Bronowski, does a knowledge of the system enable you to follow the frequency changes?"

"Certainly not. Only access to the programme will give the necessary knowledge."

"Then we need access to the programmes."

A thickset man on the Generals left spoke for the first time. "Stokowski's English friend will know the appropriate department to infiltrate."

"He will give away nothing." The General spoke with conviction.

"We have ways of persuading such people," said Colonel Ilyanovitch.

"Stokowski is not a trained agent," said the General.

"Sonia Medov is," said Colonel Ilyanovitch. "All we need from Stokowski's friend Wigmore is the appropriate military establishment responsible for setting up the programmes, then hand over to Medov. She won't need telling how to infiltrate that establishment with a mole." General Mikhailovitch kept his thoughts to himself...He would like to have suspended Ilyanovitch, but his knowledge and handling of the agents still in place was vital to the security of the Soviet Union. It was vital to know what the West was doing and saying behind the diplomacy of détente. Ilyanovitch was exploiting the situation. He had to get his Sonia out of the KGB. He had made a dangerous enemy of the man whose ambition it had been to hold the post that had fallen instead to an outsider, a hero of the hated Afghan war.

Dr. Bronowski listened appalled as the discussion progressed. A plan was proposed whereby Galya would lure Frank Wigmore away from surveillance, where he would be kidnapped and tortured, and then have his suicide arranged. He decided it was time to interject. "May I make a point, Comrade General," he said. Colonel Ilyanovitch scowled at him. The General responded immediately.

"Please do. We would welcome any help you can give us. You realise of course how vital it is to have access to the secret communications of the West."

"Of course, but knowing Galya Stokowski as I do - she has been in my department for a number of years - I do not believe she is the right person for the sort of espionage you are proposing."

"That is for us to decide," interjected Colonel Ilyanovitch. "You are here as the technical expert. When we want technical and scientific advice we will ask you. Foreign affairs and counter espionage are the responsibility of the First Chief Directorate, which is represented at this meeting. We already have the authority of the Central Committee to take any steps necessary to obtain this information. This gives us the authority to deploy our staff as we wish."

"Nevertheless," said the General quietly, "Dr. Bronowski's personal knowledge of Stokowski is extremely useful. I know from military experience that the best laid plans can go wrong if delegated incorrectly."

"I appreciate that," Comrade General. "That lesson was well learnt from our ignominious retreat from Afghanistan."

The General ignored the colonel's remark. "I propose to avoid such extreme measures. Don't forget that it is also in our interest to maintain our improving relations with the West. We have had enough of the cold war. Improved relations with the West are in our best interest. We must not jeopardise with the risk of a scandal at this juncture. Galya Stokowski is doing an excellent job in public relations as well as the task for which she was originally given. According to Comrade Medov's intelligence Wigmore's marriage is collapsing, and he may end up marrying Stokowski. This would completely change the scenario"

"Are we not in danger of letting the opportunity slip, Comrade General?" asked Colonel Ilyanovitch.

"No. I am due to go to Europe again to discuss arms limitation and mutual inspection arrangements. I will review the situation during my visit. I will be there at the time of the sailing championships and will take the opportunity to show my support and meet Frank Wigmore."

"The class of boat they are sailing is pretty insignificant," murmured Colonel Ilyanovitch. "It is not an Olympic class. I am surprised at the interest."

"Media hype can make anything interesting," responded the General, "and Galya Stokowski has turned out to be very photogenic. The yachting press have taken to her. This concludes the meeting." To emphasise the point he picked up and put away his papers. The rest of the participants took the hint and filed out of the room. Dr Bronowski, dispirited and worried, was at the door when the General called him back. "Would you care to join me for a drink, Comrade Doctor?" he asked.

"Delighted," Dr. Bronowski responded with genuine warmth. He felt an empathy with the General that he could never have felt with any of the other stony-faced apparatchiks. The General opened a cabinet and took out a bottle of scotch."

"Will whisky suit you?"

"It will indeed. An unexpected pleasure." The General handed him a glass containing a liberal portion and indicted one of the carafes of water, adding none to his. He walked over to the window and stared out, saying nothing for a while.

"I don't like it," he said at last. As Dr Bronowski was not sure what it was he didn't like, he made no response.

"Damned duplicity," continued the General, "but we have to do it. We must not be caught wrong footed. We have to know what they are thinking behind the diplomatic front."

"It is a pity we cannot have genuine co-operation," ventured Dr Bronowski.

"Exactly," said the General, "as exemplified by Stokowski and Wigmore in England. They have no wish to be caught up in a web of intrigue. They want to co-operate and are demonstrating it by example." Dr Bronowski wished there was someone else doing the co-operation. "We have to turn their activity to political advantage."

"There must be another way," said Dr Bronowski hopefully.

"I don't know of one. We really need that information."

"There is mutual trust."

"We can't afford it. I can see you don't like it either."

"I don't, but for a different reason."

"Oh?" The General looked enquiringly at Dr Bronowski. "You can be candid with me. You are from a different world, outside political intrigue."

"I would like to see Galya Stokowski back in her own country. I want her as my daughter-in-law."

CHAPTER 15

The beach to Felixtowe Ferry was a hive of industry. The road to the ferry, which ceased operations long ago, was a dead end. The Yacht club car park was full. Boats were being unloaded from their trailers onto the launching trolleys. The trailers had to be moved out of the car park to make way for more launching trolleys.

Frank and Galya had arrived early. Their boat was already on the launching trolley, and had been measured for compatibility with the class specification. They studied the course outside the starters hut. It took them out of the river, through a channel between two sand banks. The banks were well covered at high tide but would form a hazard on the ebb tide.

"The tide through that channel gets quite vicious," said Frank, studying the map of the tidal streams. "To get back into the river much after high water we will have to keep close to the edge of the channel. Let's hope we don't have to tack across it."

Galya looked at the windsock flying from the clubhouse. "We will be on a reach through the channel," she said. "Starboard out and port in. It's blowing about force 4, gusting 5 or 6. Should be quite exciting."

"It will. Most of the fireball class sail on inland water. They will have difficulty making sufficient allowance for the tide. At sea there is nothing to indicate its strength. Quite a few will get swept the wrong side of the marker buoy and will have difficulty getting back to round it."

"Look who's talking. Make sure you round all the marks after that."

"I started sailing on coastal waters. I feel at home in tidal water."

"After that uncharacteristic show of confidence let's get launched and get the feel of the boat before the start. There's over an hour. We should be able to complete a trial lap. Wasn't that why you called me at the crack of dawn?"

General Mikhailovitch, standing on the sea wall with his driver Leon, watched as they set off, Galya having to swing out on the trapeze in the freshening wind.

Also watching the boat, and the General, was David Blake. "Looks like being an interesting day," he mused.

The General looked about him to see what sort of press coverage there was. He could only see one professional looking photographer and noted with satisfaction that he had taken a couple of shots of the boat as it set off. No doubt the paper had an arrangement with the yachting journals. It was not important enough to be covered by the national press. They could rely on a report from the race organisers.

The calibre of the opposition was apparent from the start of the first race. They were almost last away, getting the dirty wind from the fleet ahead of them. They finished around the middle of the field, due only, as Frank had predicted, many of the boats underestimating the tide at the outer mark and having to tack back against wind and tide.

"We have to do better than that," complained a despondent Galya as they swung into wind at the jetty. Galya jumped out with the painter and secured it to a mooring ring. Frank let down the mainsail and secured it to the boom.

"We are up against the best helmsmen in the country, don't forget," he said. "We did well not to come last. I sailed the as well as I knew how. I just couldn't get through."

Galya knew he wanted to do well to please her. "We need to get ourselves into a good position at the start. When we get a good start we usually do well."

"I am always afraid we will jump the gun and have to go back to restart."

"I know. Is it permitted to go outside the channel?"

"We can make any course provided we round the marks in the right order."

"We can sail over the sandbanks then?"

"Certainly. We would have to be ready to lift the centre plate as soon as it touched."

"The fleet sets off on the starboard tack. We could go off from the extreme left on a port tack over the sand bank, which is already beginning to cover. This would give us clear water. They would have to tack back as they approached the opposite bank. We could come back across the fleet on starboard. They will have to give way."

"It's risky, but it's worth a try. We would really have to move to catch them coming back across the channel."

"We will miss the incoming tide over the sand bank."

"OK then. You will have to be sharp lifting the centre plate or we will capsize."

General Mikhailovitch was astounded to see Galya and Frank set off in the opposite direction to the rest of the fleet, sailing very fast to where only a few minutes before there had been waves breaking over the sand.

The boat reached the centre of the bank before the centre plate touched. "Going about," yelled Frank, pushing the tiller across and pulling in the mainsheet. Galya let go the jib sheet as she pulled the plate half way up, ducked under the boom and hurled herself across to the other side of the boat. The boat rose up and planed again, heading straight across the rest of the fleet, now on the port tack back across the channel, just as Galya had predicted.

"Starboard," yelled Frank and had the satisfaction of seeing all the leading boats give way - except one. Just one boat had been far enough ahead not to have had to alter course. Frank recognised it as THUNDERBID, the winner of the previous race. It crossed his bow with only a couple of feet to spare, but well judged – enough to avoid a protest by Frank. He was going wide of the marker buoy to approach it on starboard tack. Frank changed tack and approached close-hauled.

"We'll just about make it," called Frank."

"No, he's coming straight for us," yelled Galya. "We'll have to give way."

"Not if I'm already rounding the mark."

"Starboard," called the helmsman of THUNDERBIRD.

"Water at the mark," responded Frank as he rounded it and tacked.

"I had to alter course to avoid you," called the THUNDERBIRD helmsman. "I shall make an official protest. The crew tied a white handkerchief to one of the shrouds to indicate they were protesting.

"I was rounding the mark and was entitled to clear water," Frank called as he luffed up to prevent THUNDERBIRD from passing.

"We will let the race committee decide that," replied THUNDERBIRD'S helmsman, frustrated at not being able to overtake.

Now firmly in the lead Frank managed to hold onto it until the finish. There was no elation.

"We'll take the boat out of the water for the lunch break," said Frank as they came into the jetty. Galya jumped out and ran to fetch the launching trolley. Frank lowered the sails, stepped into the water and walked the boat to the launching ramp. Pulling the boat on the trolley a third, then a fourth pair of hands lent assistance. At the top of the ramp Galya turned to thank her helper. "Comrade General!" she exclaimed before she could check herself, going red with embarrassment, then white with fear as she realised he might be there incognito. The General saw her discomfort and laughed.

"Don't worry," he said in Russian, then for the benefit of the man helping on the other side of the boat continued in English. "I told my opposite number at the arms limitation conference that I would take the day off to watch my compatriot sailing in the national championships." He turned to Frank. "Let me introduce myself, Leo Mikhailovitch. You have made my day winning that last race."

"I am afraid we might not have won," said Galya, relieved that she had not made a gaff. "The helmsman of the following boat has protested, and if it is upheld we will be disqualified."

"I am afraid it will be upheld," said David Blake.

"How the hell do you know?" asked Frank. "Why are you always turning up like a bad penny?"

"I get no satisfaction from telling you," responded Blake. "I too got a lot of pleasure from the last race until I overheard the race officer talking about that incidence at the outer mark. Both he and the Commodore agreed that THUNDERBIRD had had to change course to avoid you and that clearly put you at fault."

"Blast," exploded Frank. "That means disqualification for sure.

"I am afraid it will." None of them had noticed the helmsman of THUNDERBIRD approach, together with the race officer.

The race officer introduced himself. "I have come to advise you," he said, "that the committee will be considering the protest at

1pm. You are invited to attend to defend the protest and to call any witnesses you wish."

"There seems little point in contesting it," said Frank despondently. "It seems we were at fault."

"That's a sensible decision," said the helmsman introducing himself as John Freeman. "No bad feeling?" He held out his hand and Frank shook it with obvious reluctance.

"What an anti-climax after all our preparation. I am sorry Galya." She turned her head away, fighting back her tears.

"I think it is time for some of your excellent English beer," said the General. "You will join us, Mr. Blake." The General grinned at the man from MI5. "Why have secrets from one another?

"Why indeed," said David Blake? "Are you enjoying your stay in Britain?"

"It is always a pleasure to visit your country. You should visit Russia some time."

"I will see if I can get on an arms limitation delegation of some sort."

"We also welcome tourists."

"I think this particular tourist would create a bit of interest in your department."

"No more interest than I create over here. I cannot imagine why you are keeping an eye on me. The purpose of my visit is quite open and has the blessing of your Ministry of Defence."

"What of your interest in Galya, and her friend Frank Wigmore."

"Is it not good to see cooperation instead of confrontation? Co-operation in sporting events is only the beginning. It leads to other things. We are co-operating in arms control and who would have thought I would be invited to observe NATO exercises, and invite your Generals to inspect our military installations."

"The trust is still lacking."

"No doubt it will follow. Caution is still called for. We have been attacked too often from the West.

They made their way to the Ferryboat Inn. Frank and David went to the crowded bar to order beer and sandwiches. Galya and the General secured a table. He talked to her in Russian putting her at her ease, and making her laugh. He reverted to English when Frank and David returned.

"Good health and better luck in the next race," said the General.

"Cheers," responded Frank, "but I am not sure it is worth it now. What do you think, Galya?"

"I too have lost enthusiasm," she said.

Frank looked at her in surprise. He had expected her to respond in her usual lively and enthusiastic way - to want to fight back. To make matters worse, John Freeman sauntered over to their table. He gave a brief nod of acknowledgment to Frank and a smile of recognition to Galya. All set for this afternoon?" he asked.

"I will probably scratch," Frank replied.

John Freeman raised his eyebrows. "So your crew will be free. How would you like to crew for me?" he asked addressing Galya without waiting for a reply from Frank. " I am afraid I don't know your name."

"Galya," she said, coming alive, "and I would love to crew for you."

"Then we had better get a little pre-race familiarisation."

"What about your regular crew?" queried Frank?

"I expect he will be glad of a break, now he knows the championship is in the bag."

"Of course," said Frank, "you are in an invulnerable position. You have only to start in the last race and the championship is yours."

"We will win the final race," said Galya, picking up the remains of her sandwich as John Freeman stood aside for her.

"You could do with another drink, Frank," said David Blake.

CHAPTER 16

Frank lost interest in the conversation between David Blake and the General. They seemed to be talking in riddles. Spy mania. He left them to it and went to his boat to prepare it for towing back to London. It would be tricky lowering the mast single-handed.

"Dad, Dad." He recognised Sally's voice and turned to see her rushing towards him. Instinctively he opened his arms to catch her swing her round and lower her gently to the ground. Galya watched them as John Freeman's boat pulled away from the jetty.

"Dad, can I crew for you in the next race? Please Dad," pleaded Sally.

"I won't be in the next race, but I'll take you for a sail if you like."

"That would be lovely. Mum said it would be no good asking you because you would be racing with that Russian."

"She will be crewing for some one else. Where's Kate?"

"She is with Mum. We have been looking all over for you. We saw your car in the car park and thought you would be going back to it for sandwiches or something."

"Your life jackets are still in the boot of the car. Here are the keys. Bring Kate's as well. I can't take one of you without the other."

"But you will take me first, won't you?"

"Yes."

"I'll tell Mum I've found you," she called as she rushed off."

It was several weeks since he had seen Edith, and then only in the solicitor's office. He wondered what sort of greeting he would get.

Sally came rushing back with the life jackets followed by Edith and their eldest daughter.

"Hi Dad," called Kate. "Long time - no see"

"Hi Kate. Hello Edith. I didn't expect to see you here." She looked vulnerable, he thought, less sure of herself outside the house where she was so bossy. She was wearing a short yellow cotton dress - no stockings. Her legs were still in good shape, he noticed. Kate had put her baseball cap on her mother's head, making her look more like her sister than her mother.

"We came to see you race. We were thrilled to see you come in first. Why aren't you sailing in this one?"

"We were disqualified."

"What! Why?"

"We should have given way at the outer maker buoy."

"What on earth for? You got there first. I was watching through binoculars."

Frank was surprised by the vehemence of her remark, not least because it was said in his defence. "The race committee thought otherwise, so I am free to take my charming daughter for a sail."

"Will she be safe?"

Frank laughed. "You don't change," he said. "I will make sure it she is safe."

Kate said she didn't want to sail. She would rather stay with her mother.

He sailed up river to keep out of the way of the race and struggled back against the incoming tide, having to spill wind in order to stop the boat from healing too much with his inexperienced crew. They got ashore in time to see the finish of the race. There were a dozen boats fighting it out to cross the finishing line, but it was THUNDERBIRD that stormed across first, with Galya out at full stretch on the trapeze. The press photographers were now very much in evidence and seemed to have no interest in any other boat or crew other than the new champion and his temporary crew - it was all the General could wish for.

Galya jumped ashore, rushed up to Frank and flung her arms around him. "What do you think of that? She said. He gave her a hug, pleased that she had regained her spirits.

Releasing her, he said, "I don't believe you have met my wife." Galya turned still beaming with pleasure at her win, and took both Edith's hands in hers. "I am so glad to meet you," she said. The warmth of her greeting and the open candour of her manner killed all the resentment and anger Edith had felt only a few moments before.

"I am pleased to meet you too. I have heard so much about you." Edith blushed as she court Frank's eye. She quickly changed the subject. "You crewed awfully well. You must be very pleased."

"It was wonderful crewing for the new champion and it was all due to Frank's kindness. He taught me all I know about sailing." Edith felt a pang of jealousy. She had never been in his boat. She had always found an excuse to refuse. To make matters worse Frank said what a good pupil she had been. He was proud of her.

Galya talked to the two girls. Sally was open and friendly. Kate, more aware of the impending divorce and the effect of Galya's influence on her father, remained aloof. Frank introduced General Michailovitch to Edith, who was suitably impressed.

David Blake had distanced himself from the small group and was observing one of the photographers who had retained an interest in Galya and had continued taking photographs, not only of her, but also of other members of the group. When he turned his camera towards him he quickly turned away. Damned if he was going to have his photograph in some Russian rogues gallery. He shook his head disapprovingly at the General, who raised his eyebrows with an air of uncomprehending innocence. David rejoined the General. "From the Tass news agency, no doubt," he said.

"I hope so," responded the General. "Russian girl crews for British National Fireball Champion may not be earth shaking, but it makes a change from the usual depressing stuff. A small token of the new relationship between East and West,"

"It would be a more meaningful token if you stopped your covert activities."

"It will take time to trust one another, and it gives you a living. I wonder how much is perpetuated by self interest - the generation of covert activities for their own sake."

"And then they go wrong and the mistrust is perpetuated."

The General laughed. "How different it would be if it was left to you and me," he said. "It is time I was going," he added, turning to Galya. "You can come back to London in my car," he said. It was an offer she could not refuse, even if she wanted to.

"We must be going too," said Edith. It will be late for Sally by the time we are home.

"Will you come back with us?" asked Sally.

"I have to tow the boat back to the club," Frank replied.

As he held the door open for Edith, she said quietly, "I have missed you, Frank.

"It was your decision," he said.

"You could come back any time." As he closed the door he could see tears in her eyes.

Frank had a lonely drive back. By the time he had returned the boat to the club and returned to the dreary room he had rented in New Southgate it was past midnight. There was a note for him. "Your friend rang. Could you ring back in the morning," it read. It was out of character for Galya to phone, although, he realised, they had made no arrangements for their next meeting. There was no longer a valid excuse for further meetings. The outlook was bleak indeed.

It was hot and humid in Moscow. Alexei was travelling by Metro to his office. He had brought a copy of Pravda at the station. In the crowded carriage there was standing room only. He kept his paper folded. Others were not so considerate. Over the shoulder of a fellow passenger he saw a banner headline "RUSSIAN GIRL CREWS FOR BRITISH SAILING CHAMPION." Below the headline was a picture of a girl hanging horizontally out from a frail looking boat, her legs bare to the thighs, her body covered in a snugly fitting wet suit, one hand extended fully above her head, the other controlling a line to the foresail. Almost obscured by the spray, as the boat skimmed over the water was a face. "Galya," he exclaimed aloud, to the astonishment of his neighbours.

He broke his journey and surprised his father in his office.

"Father, have you seen the papers this morning," he burst out with no pre-amble."

"No. Why? Has the counter-revolution started? Nobody tells me anything."

"That's not funny. According to rumours at the bank there are worrying signs of discontent at the Presidents handling of the hoped for reforms."

"Pressure from Boris Yeltsin? He is getting impatient."

"No, It is his own appointed members of the government. They want a halt to the reforms.

He ought not to go on holiday at this time. It was while Kruschev was on holiday that he was stabbed in the back by Brezhnev."

"A return to the old ways would be trouble for you?"

"Yes. I have taken a very strong line at the bank to push through a more open and free economy - enough to brand me anti-communist under earlier regimes. If the hard liners oust the President I could be in deep trouble; perhaps branded as an enemy of the people."

"I can't believe it will come to that. Don't get so involved. Leave politics to the politicians."

"That's why we are in the state we are in. It's time we stood up to them."

"It's no good standing up to them if you end up in Siberia, or worse."

"I didn't come to talk politics. Take a look at this." He handed the paper to his father. That fellow Wigmore must have won the class championship. He looks a real macho type."

"Galya looks pretty good herself."

"Too good. She looks too damned attractive in that get up, what there is of it."

"She has a good figure, hasn't she?"

"Stop getting at me. What can I do?"

"Write to congratulate her. You don't need me to tell you what to say,"

"I haven't had a reply to my last letter yet. I told her what was going on here and begged her to get back. It seems I have got my answer."

Dr. Bronowski was studying the photograph in the paper again. "The photographer was concentrating on the crew. The helmsman is

not too clear. He does not look like Wigmore
as I remember him. He is too young and it was
several years ago when I met him.”

Alexei took the paper back from his father
and started to read the text. It isn’t Wigmore,”
he said. “It is someone called John Freeman.
What is she up to out there?”

“I will have to find out.”

“How can you find out?”

“I have my sources.”

“Dad, what are you up to?”

“My visits to the First Chief Directorate are
not necessarily a one way affair.”

“Do you mean Galya is connected with the
KGB?”

“Loosely, but I hope to get her back.”

“Can you?”

“I’m working at it.”

At the sailing club on the Sunday following
the championships Galya received the praise
heaped on her with quiet modesty, pointing out
that the press had hardly mentioned John
Freeman’s regular crew. During the morning’s
race she crewed in a lack-lustre fashion, as
though her mind was elsewhere.

They did not normally visit the island on a
Sunday. Although not a rule of the club it was
tacitly considered to be out of bounds. It was
Galya’s idea that they should take their lunch
there. Frank was surprised, but realised she
would not have suggested it without a good
reason. They sailed round the back, landing out
of sight of the clubhouse and jetty.

Galya looked round at the trees, the standing on tip toe, reached above a low bough, shouted "BOO" and snatched a small microphone free from its thin connecting wires. She tossed it to Frank with a grin.

"How the devil did you know it was there?" He threw it into the lake.

Galya just smiled an enigmatic smile. She sat down and opened the plastic bag with the thick chunky sandwiches she had prepared. She looked at them with undisguised disgust and offered them to Frank. "I was told," she said in answer to Frank.

"Was it your peoples bug?"

"No. It must be connected to a small transmitter higher up in the tree. Our people could listen as well. Not very clever."

"It's just as well I didn't seduce you."

"Yes. I wouldn't have let you. You would probably have been arrested to prevent blackmail. You would have been responsible for maintenance if it had resulted in a pregnancy. That is the law in Russia."

"I'll remember that. What about the handsome Mr. Freeman? Did he make a pass at you?"

"He certainly did." She smiled mischievously. "I discovered he was not involved in secret defence work, so I declined his approaches."

"Cat."

She paused. "This is not what I came to talk about, Frank. I don't know quite how to say this. It is as if an era is coming to an end."

"You are going back to Moscow."

"It had to come one day, Frank."

"Yes. I suppose so. I can't persuade you to stay?"

Galya hesitated. "My mind is made up; or perhaps I should say it has been made up for me. It comes to the same thing."

"When do you go?"

"In about ten days. There are a few things to clear up, then I shall be working under Dr. Bronowski again."

"Won't you find that a bit dull now?"

"I don't think so."

"Are you being sent back because you failed to get the information that was requested?"

She smiled. "I might have got it."

"What do you mean?"

"I will tell you. You can have this information as a bonus. A sort of one way traffic."

"Don't tell me anything you shouldn't. You know I couldn't reciprocate."

"It is of no consequence. It doesn't matter about frequency agile communications anymore. I have found out all I need to know by my own efforts. I am an engineer too don't forget."

"And a damned good one by the sound of it."

"A very good one. I did a few sums and came up with some interesting answers. Frequency agile communications has no strategic importance. It was only intended for radio communications and due to antenna configuration difficulties, it can only be used over short distances."

"I knew that. It is what my field trials indicated."

"Now I have proved it. I have passed my work on and it has been accepted. It has also been accepted that I would be of more use to Dr. Bronowski than on a purchasing mission over here. I think General Michailovitch has had something to do with it. He seems to know Dr. Bronowski. He wants the new look Soviet Union working and co-operating with the West. He has met President Gorbachev several times. They must have hit it off – been on the same wavelength is your expression, I think."

"So you think Gorbachev really wants to change the Soviet system."

"To some extent. He wants it both ways. He feels an allegiance to the party, the Communist party. The party is opposed to change. Sooner or later something has to give. We are at a crossroads. Things are happening in my country. That is why I want to get back there. I want to be involved, not on the sidelines."

"I shall miss you." Galya kissed him. Frank folded her in his arms and they held each other tight for a few moments. "Darling Galya I really will miss you. Can't I persuade you to stay?"

She pressed closer to him. You almost have. We will come back here just one more time," she whispered.

"We used to come on a Monday. That means tomorrow."

"OK. Same place, same time."

She wants me, he realised, wants me to make love to her.

They skipped the next race and watched it from a secluded spot on the bank. It was a balmy afternoon, warm, with very little wind. The boats were hardly moving, some completely becalmed. Galya appeared to have gone to sleep. She half opened her eyes. "Frank," she murmured, "I have deceived you."

"Oh?"

"I didn't say anything that wasn't true."

"Then how could you have deceived me?"

"What I told you was not only for your ears."

"How do you mean? There was nobody else listening. You had disconnected the radio bug."

"There was another one. I didn't see it, but I know it was there. It was a back up tape recorder. Your people expected we might find the radio bug. They reasoned that if we did we would feel a sense of false security and let out something we didn't want them to hear, so I let out something I wanted them to hear. It confirmed that you were clean. Had you said anything that would have made them think otherwise I would have located and destroyed the recorder?"

"You never cease to amaze me."

"I amaze myself sometimes. I have missed my vocation. I would have made a very good spy."

"You would have made a very good anything."

"Flattery will get you nowhere." Or will it?

CHAPTER 18

The sails of the few boats that had started in the afternoon race went limp. The starters hooter went and his pennant lowered. The afternoon's race was abandoned. The peace was shattered as the boats and their crews came ashore.

Galya opened her eyes, blinked and looked at all the sudden activity. Frank looked down at her. "You looked so peaceful," he said.

"I was. I don't want the day to end, but I suppose we had better make a move."

"The day hasn't ended yet. We'll take a run out to Henley. There's a wonderful place by the river. We'll wine and dine there."

"Sound's heavenly."

Frank avoided the Motorway, taking a slow country route. He felt a little romantic music would be in order and selected the appropriate station on the radio. They drove in silence for a while.

The music was broken by the four-o-clock news. Frank reached to turn it off. He did not turn it off. "President Gorbachev has been replaced by his deputy," said the announcer.

"Oh no," gasped Galya. Frank turned up the volume and raised his eyebrows. "It could not be worse. They are hard liners. With control of the KGB and the army they will revert to all the old practises. All hope of a freer society promised by President Gorbachev will be nothing but a dream." She could have added that Ivan Ilyanovitch would also be among the new leaders, probably taking over from General. Mikhailovitch. "Oh my God," she said aloud. "I must get back to Sonia. Please take me back to the flat."

Frank turned back and put his foot down. He screeched to a halt at the flat and followed Galya into it. Sonia, ashen white, was standing by the phone. She turned to Galya. "They've arrested him. It's Ivan's doing. I'll kill him. I'll kill the bastard."

"Sonia, it might blow over."

"It's too late," Sonia hissed. "You know what they do when they want to disgrace someone." Galya didn't know, but the tone of Sonia's voice left little to the imagination. "Ivan will be in it. It's just what he's been waiting for. There will be no stopping him. I'll stop him. They showed me how to kill an enemy of the people. Once it was decided he was as good as dead. Ivan Ilyanovitch is as good as dead."

They had been speaking in Russian, but Frank was getting the idea of the violence of Sonia's reaction. "The phone," he whispered to Galya. She looked at it in horror. And rushed to the kitchen, rustled in a drawer and threw Frank a screwdriver. He unscrewed the base and removed a silicon chip connected to the incoming cable. He raised his eyebrows to Sonia. "Friend or foe?" he asked.

"Ours. It means I've no time to waste." She reverted to Russian again. "I have a priority ticket and the necessary documents ready to use in case I ever needed to make an emergency getaway. Now is the time to use them."

"What about at the other end?" Galya asked desperately.

"My KGB identification will get me anywhere in Russia." This admission of KGB involvement Galya thought wise to let pass with no comment.

"It will be dangerous for you now you have crossed Ilyanovitch."

"He will be too busy looking after number one to expect me back so soon."

"Please don't go. Frank can arrange political asylum through his contact."

"No. That is for you. Good luck. Perhaps we shall meet again, but I doubt it." She picked up her ready-made bag and rushed out of the door.

Galya stood staring after her. Frank felt awkward. For want of something better to say he mumbled, "Sonia seems capable of looking after herself."

"She can't take on the whole of the KGB single handed. What can I do?" She paused. "I wonder if there is any more news." Frank switched on the radio. "They are telling us nothing new."

"That correspondent was on the phone from Moscow," said Frank

"The phone. You would have thought they would have cut communication to the outside world. Sonia was able to phone. There is hope yet. If the coup succeeds Sonia is going to need political asylum. Her life won't be worth living over there."

"How can you get her back now?"

"It is too complicated to explain. Can you contact your man and make arrangements on her behalf. She is against the new government and her life is in danger. That should mean refugee status."

"And you? The same applies, surely."

"No. It won't be necessary for me," she said. Go to your contact now while I do some phoning.

"Frank left the flat and walked straight to the blue Cortina parked a few yards down the road. He opened the passenger door and got in beside the driver. "Take me to David Blake." The driver looked at him with apparent incomprehension. "Oh for heaven's sake stop play acting. You know damn well who I am and who David Blake is."

"OK, OK." He was a man of indefinite age, probably not much more than thirty, pasty faced, overweight and smelling of stale cigarette smoke. He took a cigarette out of a packet on the dashboard and proceeded to light it. As an afterthought he grunted, "smoke?"

"No thank you."

"Where was Medov off to then?"

"Why didn't you follow her?"

"I ask the questions."

"You won't get the answers. David Blake will – if we ever get there."

"The driver put the car in gear and moved off. He picked up a microphone from a hook under the dash and gave a call sign, which was acknowledged. "Got a passenger" was all he said." He drove in silence to Whitehall and pulled up in a side road beside the Foreign Office. "Come to reception," he said as he got out of the car. Frank followed him. Any grandeur suggested from the outside stopped as soon as you stepped inside. Why did all Civil Service reception areas look so melancholy? Abandon hope all ye that enter here should be the message in place of "ALL VISITERS PLEASE REPORT TO RECEPTION. The scruffy driver picked up the telephone handset from the desk and spoke briefly. He nodded to the reception desk and left the building.

The elderly security officer at the desk pushed a small duplicate passbook to him. Name, address and nationality. It must be signed by Mr. Blake and make sure you hand it in before you leave." He motioned to a middle-aged lady reading a magazine behind him. "Room 304, Mr. Blake," he said.

Frank followed her to the lift, which took them to the third floor. She knocked at the door of room 304.

"Come in," called David Blake. Frank found himself in a sparsely furnished office, with plain drab beige walls. David Blake was sitting at an empty desk. This was obviously not Blake's office – simply a convenient interview room. Their conversation would probably be recorded – not that he cared.

"So you cadged a lift with my man."

"It seemed the most convenient way of finding you."

"Now that you have found me, what have you to tell me?"

"General Michailovitch has been arrested."

"That is news to me, and bad news too. Have you heard anything of a man called Ilyanovitch, Ivan Ilyanovitch, a colonel I believe?"

"Yes. It is believed he would have been associated with the plot and promoted. Sonia Medov believes him to have been responsible for the General's arrest."

"That would not surprise me."

"It is something else that brought me here. It is connected to the Russian coup. Galya Stokowski believes her friend and boss to be in some kind of danger from this fellow Ilyanovitch. She asked if I could set the wheels in motion for political asylum for her."

"Well, well." David Blake fumbled in his pocket for his pipe he put it on the table, realised he had no tobacco with him and put it back in his pocket. "And what of your friend Stokowski?"

"I'm not sure."

David Blake gave him a searching look. "Surely," he said, "you knew that Stokowski had made an enemy of Ilyanovitch."

"I didn't know. How do you know?"

David Blake chuckled. "For some reason best known to themselves the Ruskies bugged the flat. That was perfect for us. We had only to tap the telephone line and we had access as well - very convenient."

Frank looked aghast. "Yes Frank we did hear Stokowski ask for information, and we heard you refuse. That is why we didn't lean on you too much. It didn't suit Ilyanovitch though. He demanded action. He pressurised Stokowski and got a bloody nose for his trouble. Only the intervention of the General saved her from the dire consequences of assaulting her superior."

"She can't possibly go back to Russia now General Mikhailovitch has been arrested. I can't understand why she only asked for asylum for Sonia Medov. She is on her way to Moscow."

David Blake pulled out his pipe again, then remembering the tobacco situation, put it back in his pocket. "She obviously has some plan to get Medov back here. As for herself, it is my view that she wants to get back to carry on the fight against the new regime – underground if necessary. She is quite a girl, your Galya. He paused. "With the Prime Minister and the United States President talking to and supporting Boris Yeltsin I consider your two friends should be supported and you can tell Galya Stokowski that I will do all I can for Medov, but I can't promise anything." He fished an envelope out of his pocket, removed the contents and scribbled a number on the back. "You can always leave a message on that number," he said. "It won't be any good looking for any more free rides. I am removing your surveillance. We are short staffed and not the treasury's favourite people at the moment."

"And you won't be able to listen to our telephone conversations any more," said Frank, fishing the telephone bug from his pocket and tossing it on the table.

Galya had had no luck with her 'phoning. Dr. Bronowski was out of the office. "We think

he has gone to the Parliament building,"
confided one of his colleagues. Galya gritted
her teeth and rang a number she knew she
should have rung days ago. It was closed due to
the emergency.

She recalled the confidence the General
placed in his chauffeur. It was possible he
might have returned to the General's flat to
salvage private papers. She found the number
in Sonia's notebook. Leon answered and
listened to her story.

CHAPTER 19

There were not many females who had KGB identity cards. The official at Moscow Airport could not recall having seen one before, but the last thing he wanted in the present uncertain climate was a brush with that particular organisation. He looked at her passport, looked at Sonia Medov, looked at her photograph, looked at her KGB identity card and after a moment's hesitation let her through. She had not doubted for a moment that it would not be so.

No point in wasting time. It was nearly evening. She would catch her quarry at his apartment, which for the elite was within the compound of the First Chief Directorate of the KGB. She had a quick look in her handbag to reassure herself the small plastic handgun was still in place. It had escaped the attention of the metal detectors at both ends of her journey just as intended. It was lethal at close range, which was exactly the way it would be used. It was also comparatively silent. She might be able to get away undetected, not that she was worried about that; the assassination was all. She took a taxi to Yasenov, the headquarters of the First Chief Directorate.

"It is lucky it is on the ring road," the driver said. "I would not drive into central Moscow for anyone, not even you."

"Why not?"

"Too many tanks," he replied.

Tanks would be a minor hazard compared to the next hazard she had to surmount – gaining entry into the compound of The First Chief Directorate. The taxi was not allowed past the entrance gate on the ring road. Her pass would lose its magic here. It might get her through the main gate, but not into the main building, but it was not the main building she needed, it was the accommodation block. Would she be recognised? Would it be an advantage if she were recognised? She had been well known to the security staff years ago. They would wonder what she was doing back after years of absence. They might even contact Ivan Ilyanovitch to check.

She found out soon enough. She was recognised by the officer at the entrance security office.

"Delighted to see you back," he beamed. She gave him her most brilliant smile, somewhat surprised at his effusive welcome. She suspected, quite rightly that he was insuring his position with all and sundry. One never knew who was friend or foe – best not to step on anybodies toes. He pushed a large book towards her. It recorded everyone who entered the premises. Only the directors were exempt from signing. The security guards recorded their arrival.

For the first time Sonia felt real fear. She was trapped now. Only a fast exit before the assassination was discovered and an escape from the country could save her. She made her way to the Dacha complex. She would need to pass the scrutiny of the house manageress, who she recalled always looked down her nose at her, well knowing the purpose of her visits. In the event the past was a blessing. The formidable lady assumed her visit was no different from the earlier ones. "Come to celebrate his promotion?" she enquired?"

Sonia was taken off guard. "Promotion'?"

"Didn't he tell you? It's Lieutenant General Ilyanovitch now. He will soon be moving into a more prestigious apartment."

"That will be nice," responded Sonia, recovering her poise, but feeling less and less confident. The building was deathly quiet.

"I am surprised you are not watching the events in Moscow on television," Sonia said hopefully.

"There is a news blackout. Surely you knew."

"I have only just got back from London," Sonia said. "I am hoping Comrade Ilyanovitch will bring me up to date on the situation."

"I don't recall him coming in. He has been working very late recently."

"Then I will wait for him in his apartment. Perhaps you could let me have a key." It was a gamble.

The house manageress was not too sure. She should refuse to let anyone have the spare key; but Sonia was not anybody. She was the General's mistress. The last person she wanted to cross was Comrade General Ilyanovitch. She gave Sonia the key.

There was no escape now. Perhaps she should not have been so hasty. Undue haste was contrary to her training. She should have waited and planned for a more opportune moment" somewhere different from the very centre of the security network. She would never get away with it, not that she had ever thought that she would. There was no other opportunity. It was now or never. She was committed there was no going back. The silence in the building was getting to her. She would switch on the radio when she was in the room. It would drown the noise of the supposedly quiet pistol. They were new. Ivan had sent it to her in the diplomatic bag. "You might need it some day," he had said. She had never heard one fired. She would not be able to switch on the radio. It would alert her quarry. Perhaps he would be alerted by the house manager. Perhaps he was already in the room after all.

She removed the gun from her bag, slipped off the safety catch and held it ready in her right hand. She put the strap of her bag over her shoulder and gently eased the key into the lock. When it was fully home she turned it sharply, pushing the door open and stepped quickly into the room. It appeared empty. She let out her breath in relief, then her arms were pinned to her side and a hand clapped over her mouth.

CHAPTER 20

Frank spent Tuesday in the office, unable to concentrate. He felt tied in with the events in the Soviet Union. Galya was in danger and was ignoring that danger.

His colleagues at work wanted to discuss the situation with him, but he could not. He told his secretary he was catching up with a backlog of work and was not to be disturbed. In fact he worked to kill time before he was able to 'phone Galya at her flat at five. She answered.

"Can I come over?" he asked.

"Please, as soon as you can," she pleaded.

At the flat he took Galya in his arms and held her until the tension had eased.

"It's awful at the trade mission," she said.

"Tell me."

"It's obvious nobody welcomes the coup, but they daren't say so. They ask me where Sonia is. I say she has returned to Moscow to be briefed on the new situation and how it relates to the work over here. They don't believe me. They seem to think I am an informer, not only to Sonia but also to her boss. He puts the fear of god into them. But it is Sonia I am really worried about."

Frank went into the kitchen and poured a large gin and tonic for Galya and got a beer for himself. "We'll go out for a meal," he said.

"No. I want to stay in the flat. Sonia might 'phone and I want to hear if Leon Ivanov got to the airport in time to catch her. When she said she would kill Ilyanovitch I think she really meant it."

"I don't know much about him but he sounds a nasty bit of work. I hear you had a bit of a fracas with him. You never told me about that."

"How did you hear?"

"I didn't hear. David Blake did. I didn't tell you all last night. You had other things on your mind."

"Tell me now."

Frank told her.

"It is as dangerous for you to go back to Moscow as it is for Sonia," Frank continued. "You said yourself that Ilyanovitch would probably take over the powerful Active Measures Directorate. He is unlikely to forget or forgive his humiliation. He wasted no time acting against his former boss. He will be after you."

"He will have other things on his mind. I will be out of his way with Dr. Bronowski. I think he will want to forget our little incident."

"Is it worth the risk?"

"I don't think you understand. I love my country. I know it has been badly governed. It was badly governed under the Tsars as well. That was why they were overthrown. The wrong people took over, just as they are doing now. It is up to everyone, including me, to see that it does not happen again."

"So why not wait here in safety until after the counter coup."

"To come out of hiding when all the other people have taken all the risks?"

"You are more vulnerable."

"No, the people holding out in the parliament building are more vulnerable. Didn't you here the news. Boris Yeltsin climbed onto an army tank to declare his opposition to the new regime. The army might have shot him. You have no idea what it is like to see your country torn apart."

"I am learning fast. I really believed that given the choice you would prefer the West than in the Soviet Union with all its hardships."

"You deceived yourself. Democracy is better than dictatorship; but the party system as practised here is pretty rotten. I would hope we could do better."

"What is wrong with the Mother of Parliaments?"

"Party dogma rules."

The telephone rang. Galya answered. Frank saw her look of astonishment as she exclaimed in Russian: "Comrade General! We heard you had been arrested."

"So I was," he replied. "The officers who arrested me defected to Yeltsin, so we all went to the Parliament buildings instead of the KGB headquarters. Can I talk to Sonia?"

Galya went white. "She is in Moscow Comrade General."

"Where!"

Galya gave him the details.

CHAPTER 21

Ivan Ilyanovitch felt triumphant. The power was back where it belonged. He and other like minded party members were-establishing the old order, where the word of the party was law - no questions asked.

He stretched his legs, luxuriating in the back of a large black bulletproof limousine, a symbol of his new status of lieutenant General, a rank that had been conferred on him by the central committee in recognition of his long and unstinting service in upholding the best traditions of the KGB. In addition he had been appointed head of the Department of Administrative Organs, its purpose to supervise the appointments and functions of the KGB. His brief was to rid it of all elements not sympathetic to the new regime and to promote the traditional role of the KGB as the guardian of socialism.

He had wasted no time in implementing his responsibilities. First on his list had been Lieutenant General Mikhailovitch. While the newly appointed General would occupy an office compatible with his status in the Lubranka, the KGB headquarters in Dzerzhinski Square, Comrade General Mikhailovitch would languish in the prison in the basement with other enemies of the people to confess to their activities undermining the Communist Party.

He was on his way back to his apartment in Yasenev. He would soon be in an apartment more suited to his new status. Perhaps he could take over his old bosses apartment. He would not need it any more. The thought pleased him. He was on his way up at last, noticed by the top people.

After ratification of his new appointment he had been invited for a drink with the new President in the General Secretary's office; a rare privilege. Drink had been flowing freely before his arrival.

A heavy drinker himself, he had nonetheless been shocked by the state of his new superiors. They appeared to be drinking themselves into a drunken stupor. He was congratulated on his new appointment and told that all opposition to the new order was to be eliminated. He assured them that he would not spare himself on behalf of the party and to restore it to its rightful dominance once again. He excused himself on the basis that there was a lot to be done

His exaltation had turned to alarm. Had the plotters taken fright? It was up to the forces of law and order to take charge. He would see that they did just that, and that the credit was placed where it belonged.

As his car left the headquarters building he looked up at the statue of Felix Dzerzinsky, creator of the Cheka, the original political police organisation from which the all-powerful KGB had its origins.

"I intend to lead a force beyond that great man's wildest dreams," mused the mildly intoxicated General. His one regret was that he would be going back to an apartment that needed a woman's presence. He scowled, remembering Sonia Medov. She too would have to suffer. He would order her return and arrest. Her interrogation would be most unpleasant. She would wish she were dead.

Sonia froze in fear as a voice whispered in her ear, "First you had better drop that little gun." She dropped it. "Now don't make a sound. I am going to release you." Trembling with fear she turned round. "Just as well you weren't assigned to active measures, Comrade Medov."

She stared in disbelief as Leon quietly closed the door. "How…how did you get in," she stammered.

The same way as you, I imagine. I signed in as General Mikhailovitch's driver. They weren't to know he had been arrested.

"That's Ivan Ilyanovitch's doing," she hissed. "I'll kill him. I'll kill him."

"No need. Comrade Mikhailovitch is with Boris Yeltsin outside the Parliament building. Yeltsin is staging a counter coup, and looks like succeeding."

"I don't believe it"

"You had better believe it, for your own sake"

"How do you know? Have you seen Leo?"

"No. I was going to join him. I was in his apartment collecting some confidential papers for him, not knowing that an arrest warrant had been issued for him. Galya Stokowski phoned to warn the Comrade Mikhailovitch of your return. She had guessed your intentions. I headed for the airport to intercept you. The road was blocked by army personnel carriers and tanks, so I headed for the ring road, which was lucky for you."

"I don't understand. How can Leo be with Boris Yeltsin if he was arrested?"

"One of the young arresting officers returned to the apartment just after Stokowski's 'phone call. Comrade Michailovitch persuaded them to change sides, so instead of taking him to the KGB cells they joined Yeltsin outside the Parliament building. The officer told me I was to join Comrade Michailovitch in Leningrad, where he is to support the local government in the counter revolution."

"I must get to Leningrad - now."

"Then you had better come with me. We will wait till that old dragon downstairs has to attend to the call of nature. She does not know I am here."

Sonia intervened. She was recovering her poise. "Ivan could return at any minute," she said. "The housekeeper will tell her I am here. He will come prepared."

"True. You go down and engage the dragon in conversation. Say you can't wait any longer. I will slip out the way I came in and meet you in the car park."

Sonia held up her hand. "Listen," she said. There was the sound of voices downstairs.

"Trust me" Leon whispered. "He will only expect to see you. Stand over there as he comes in the door. Leave the rest to me." There was no time for argument. She waited. The door swung open, but Ivan stepped back out of sight, expecting a bullet. There was no bullet. He held a mirror out and saw Sonia standing empty handed on the far side of the room. He entered, revolver in hand. Sonia didn't move.

"So," he said, "you have returned. Now Comrade Mikhailovitch can no longer protect you come crawling back to me." He took a step towards her.

Leon's open palm descended like a sledgehammer on Ilyanovitch's left shoulder. There was a grunt and the newly appointed General collapsed to the floor, the revolver clattering down beside him.

"Quick, sheets and pillow cases," Leon whispered. Sonia rushed to the bedroom next door tore off a pillowcase and tossed it to Leon to twist and tie Ilyanovitch's hands behind him while Sonia used another to use as a gag. He started to groan. Leon gave him another mighty chop at the base of the neck. After they had finished trussing him up Leon reckoned it would be several hours before the alarm was raised. Meet me at the Garage and Technical Services Building. That is where I am supposed to be. I will leave by the lavatory window, the way I got in, while you make your excuses to the house manager. We will sign out together. I will say I am taking you back to your apartment."

"I haven't got an apartment."

"All the better. They will waste time looking for it."

"Comrade Medov," said Leon, when they were safely back on the ring road, "you have two alternatives. There is still time to get you back to the airport and on a flight to London before you are on the KGB wanted list. Galya Stokowski said she was arranging political asylum for you. You are in great danger here.

Or you can take a chance and come with me to Leningrad working with my boss and the opposition to the coup that is growing across the country."

"There is no question. I will join Leo and get promoted."

"Promoted?"

"To wife and mother."

CHAPTER 22

"It seems obvious," said Galya, "that the leaders are not in full control."

"They're certainly not controlling the media or communications," agreed Frank.

They were sitting in the flat waiting for news of Sonia. It was three days since she had left.

"They control the bureaucracy but not the people," continued Galya. It will collapse. It may be too late for Sonia. I am surprised we haven't heard from Ilyanovitch. We are rudderless at the trade mission. No one knows what to do, so nothing is done. That way you can do nothing wrong. I have no rapport with them. I have had my instructions. I return to Dr. Bronowski. I leave next week."

"I still think you should stay."

"I must go back Frank."

He was silent. Their relationship had changed. She still seemed to need his company, but there it stopped. Galya was very conscious of the letter she had tucked into her handbag.

The telephone rang.

"Sonia! Where are you? Leningrad...OK St. Petersburg. Are you still my boss?...My arrangements to return are complete...Yes of course I will be a bridesmaid. No, I didn't think you would get married in white. Red would be more appropriate – very patriotic...Goodbye."

They had been speaking in Russian, but Frank had picked up the relevant words. "So Sonia is in Leningrad," he said.

"St Petersburg," Galya laughed. She had come back to life. She bent over to kiss him, then slipped away from him, her eyes mocking him. "Time for a drink," she said, "and tonight I will accept your offer to eat out. Somewhere good."

"OK. Now tell me what Sonia had to say."

She handed him a whisky and poured a generous gin and tonic for herself. She sat at the table facing him.

"The coup has collapsed. President Gorbachev is returning to Moscow. She doubts if we will ever see or hear from Ivan Ilyanovitch again. She's getting married next month and I am suddenly hungry, so drink up and let's go.

Capriani's restaurant was not all that good. However, it was clean, quiet and adequate. The waiters were friendly and attentive without being overbearing. The tables were well spaced. The restaurant was busy but not packed. Altogether a good choice, they concluded

It was at the desert course, and after she had fortified herself with the excellent house wine, that Galya broached the subject she had been wrestling with for the past few days. They were discussing the future of the Soviet Union.

"It will be chaotic out there." Frank said.

"Anarchy might be a better word. President Gorbachev is unlikely to hold the states together now. There will be ethnic violence. Look what happened in Yugoslavia."

"So why go back to all that." He held up his hand to stop her interjection. "I know," he said. "I suppose if my country was in danger I would feel the same. Our parents did."

"It's more than that Frank. There is something I must tell you. Before I left Moscow, I promised someone I would return. At the time it was a light-hearted comment – a sort of throwaway line as I was leaving. It is no longer a light-hearted matter. I have been torn in two. At one point I really might be tempted to stay. The sailing was fun – the excitement, the anticipation, the challenge and you. When I heard of the coup I knew I would return. There was doubt no longer."

"What of this someone you gave your promise to?"

"Alexei, Dr. Bronowski's son. He has asked me to marry him."

"And will you?"

"Yes."

The departure area at Heathrow is a soulless place.

"That's my flight they are calling," said Galya

Frank walked with her to the departure door. She raised herself on tiptoe, kissed him lightly on the lips turned and went through the passenger's only door. Frank stood staring after her.

There was a tap on his shoulder. "Surprising who you meet at an airport," said David Blake.

"What the devil are you doing here?"

"The same as your friend. I am going to Moscow."

Frank stared at him in disbelief.

"We have been asked to a conference of security experts to discuss cooperation in the combating of terrorism, drug traffic and international crime in General. What of you Frank?"

"I'm going home."

www.ingramcontent.com/pod-product-compliance
Lightning Source LLC
Chambersburg PA
CBHW061537120726
48001CB00004B/1600